The Dog It Was That Died

and Other Plays

TOM STOPPARD

The Dog It Was That Died

and Other Plays

faber and faber

LONDON·BOSTON

First published in 1983
by Faber and Faber Limited
3 Queen Square London WC1N 3ALU
Typeset in Great Britain by
Goodfellow & Egan Limited Cambridge
Printed in Great Britain by
Whitstable Litho Whitstable Kent
All rights reserved

All rights whatsoever in these plays are strictly reserved and
professional applications for permission to perform them,
etc., must be made in advance, before rehearsals begin, to
Fraser and Dunlop (Scripts) Ltd, of 91 Regent Street,
London W1; amateur applications for permission to
perform them must be made in advance, before rehearsals
begin, to Samuel French Ltd, of 26 Southampton Street,
London WC2.

British Library Cataloguing in Publication Data

Stoppard, Tom
    The dog it was that died and other plays.
    I. Title
    822'.914   PR6069.T6

    ISBN 0-571-11984-0
    ISBN 0-571-13183-2 Pbk

Library of Congress Data has been applied for.

Contents

Introduction

Apart from the title play, which dates from last year, all these plays were written in the mid-1960s.

The Dissolution of Dominic Boot and *'M' is for Moon Among Other Things* (my idea of what makes a good title has changed since then) were written for a BBC series of fifteen-minute radio plays, *Just Before Midnight*, in early 1964. The peg for *Dominic Boot*—a man riding around in a taxi trying to raise the money he needs to catch up with the meter—is the only self-propelled idea-for-a-play I ever had and I think I wrote it in a day. *'M' is for Moon* started off as a short story which I submitted with two others to Faber and Faber in 1962 for *Introduction II: Stories by New Writers*. The other two stories and a third one got into the book but this one was rightly rejected. I remember the time of its appearance in radio-play form mainly because it received a passing favourable mention in the *Sunday Times* on a day when (riding on the top deck of a bus along Ladbroke Grove) my confidence had dipped to zero. I got on the bus a writer without hope and got off the bus feeling I could write anything. Ever since then, when asked whether critics are 'important' I think of myself dejectedly opening the *Sunday Times* on a bus.

A Separate Peace (1965) was one half of an hour-long television programme consisting of a documentary and a play which in some unspecified way were supposed to illuminate each other. The documentary which I made with Christopher Martin was about chess players. The play, which is about a man escaping from the world (into hospital), does not in fact illuminate what I think about chess players, in whom aggression is probably more important than a desire to escape, but I persuaded myself that this, the only idea I had at the time for a play, fitted well enough; and later, writing *Travesties*, I learned that Lenin denied himself chess because it distracted him from the task of changing the world.

The main significance of *Teeth* (1966) for me is that it introduced me to John Stride and John Wood who played the patient and the dentist and later played Rosencrantz and Guildenstern (though not together; the one in London, the other in New York).

Another Moon Called Earth (1967) (another of those titles) contributed a good deal to *Jumpers*: a woman who won't get out of bed, a husband working in the next room, a death, a visiting detective. Penelope in this play pushed Pinkerton out of the window and I began *Jumpers* thinking that Dottie was going to be the murderer of McFee, but I got too fond of her and ended up by trying to make a virtue of not declaring who-dun-it.

Although it doesn't help the play to know this, *Neutral Ground* closely follows the *Philoctetes* of Sophocles with variations from the Euripides version (which only survives in description). Granada TV floated the idea of a series based on myths and legends. I did not know the Sophocles play but I knew about Philoctetes from Edmund Wilson's essay 'The Wound and the Bow', and *Neutral Ground* is a reminder that most people writing for a living sometimes hustle for work. I hustled my way into a commission, selling the potency of the Philoctetes myth and then concocting a plot out of Sophocles and John le Carré. The series never happened because not enough of the commissioned plays found favour. Three years later *Neutral Ground* was taken off the shelf and produced, somewhat to my dismay, as a single play, the only vestige of the series idea being the hero's egregious name of Philo. The last third of the play was written one Sunday and the hand itches for the blue pencil in the descriptive speeches; in fact, all over the place, and not just in *Neutral Ground*. But it's too late now.

This volume is dedicated to Richard Imison, now Script Editor, Drama Radio, who liked my two unsolicited fifteen-minute plays and called me in for the first of a series of fruitful meetings which so far have produced six radio plays, ending up with *The Dog It Was That Died*.

TOM STOPPARD
August 1983

The Dog It Was That Died

A Play for Radio

Characters

RUPERT PURVIS
GILES BLAIR
HOGBIN
SLACK
PAMELA BLAIR
MRS RYAN
COMMODORE ARLON
MATRON
DR SEDDON
VICAR
CHIEF
WREN

SCENE 1

Exterior. City. Night.

PURVIS'*s footsteps on the pavement. An occasional vehicle passing, not very close.*

PURVIS *is coming up to retirement age. As he walks he is singing quietly, disjointedly, cheerfully . . . songs of farewell: the one beginning* 'Goodbye–ee . . . ' *. . . and* 'Goodbye, Piccadilly . . . ' *. . . and* 'We Don't Want to Leave You but . . . '

This singing voice is the same time and place as the footsteps and the traffic. Over this is PURVIS'*s own voice reading through a letter he has written. The singing voice and the footsteps, together with the occasional road and river traffic, continue intermittently underneath.*

PURVIS: (*Voice over*) Dear Blair. I have decided I have had enough of
  this game and I'm getting out but before I take the
  plunge . . . (PURVIS *chuckles briefly but pulls himself
  together*) . . . before I take the plunge I thought I'd give you a tip
  which if you handle it right could put you in the top spot in the
  Department, assuming that that is what you want. I have no
  fastidious scruples myself about the Chief having an opium den
  in his house in Eaton Square—perhaps that is something more of
  us should be doing—but I dare say the Prime Minister would
  take a different view. That was the tip, by the way. I wish I had
  something more on him to give you but gone are the days when a
  man could be brought down by being named in the divorce
  courts, even for sexual misconduct with the wife of a
  subordinate, and I only mention it now because your good lady
  (is she called Pamela?—I only met her once) may have been
  pulling the wool over your eyes and you have always been more

than decent to me. So you will have to do what you can with the opium den, and my only regret is that I won't be here to enjoy the brouhaha . . . .

(*The here-and-now* PURVIS *adds a few ha-has to that one.*)
Actually, it's not my *only* regret because I was looking forward to taking a belly dancer to Buckingham Palace—if the invitation was anything to do with you, many thanks for the thought. She's a splendid girl, and would have made a bit of a splash. But now it's left to me to do that. Thanks, anyway. There's something of mine which has been in the family for ages and as I'm the last of the line you may like to have it. It's supposed to have belonged to a one-legged sea captain who inspired the character of Long John Silver and I thought you might find a place for it in your folly. In all honesty, I saw one just like it on a piano in the trophy room at Cork Castle or somewhere, which gives one pause for thought, but I'll send it round anyway.

(PURVIS *is now walking across a bridge over the Thames (Chelsea Bridge) and Big Ben is heard distantly striking the quarter hour.*)
Well, I think that's about all. I hope I won't be bobbing up again so there shouldn't be any problem about the remains. I have left enough in the kitty for a plaque on the wall of St Luke's where I am church warden, and I would be grateful if you could make sure this is done. The vicar bears a grudge against me but if he starts making trouble you can take it from me that on the subject of that savoury business the choir is lying its head off man and boy, especially Hoskins, third from the end with the eyelashes. An inquiry would clear my name but I have no wish to see the diocese dragged through the mud. That is a fate I have reserved for—yours ever, Rupert Purvis.

(*Now speaking 'live'*) Well, this seems to be about the middle . . . if I can manage the parapet . . . (*He grunts and heaves himself up*) . . . I'm too old for this game . . . nice breeze anyway . . . quiet as the grave and black as your hat— to hell with the lot of them, oh dear me . . . (*He starts to sniffle, all cheerfulness gone*) . . . never mind, it's all over now. Off I . . . go . . .

(*The last word is extended with* PURVIS'*s plunge, which ends unexpectedly with the sound of a quite large dog in sudden and short-lived pain.)*

SCENE 2

*Exterior.   City park (St James's Park).   Daytime.
Big Ben is striking ten.*

BLAIR *is middle-aged and a gentleman.* HOGBIN *is younger and perhaps less of a gentleman.*

BLAIR: Good morning. On the dot.

HOGBIN: I see the tulips are in glorious bloom.

BLAIR: Absolutely. What can I do for you, Hogbin?

HOGBIN: I'm sorry—do we know each other?

BLAIR: I prefer thingummies myself. What's all this about?

HOGBIN: I see the tulips are in glorious bloom.

BLAIR: So you said. I prefer hollyhocks myself. (*Pause.*) Hibiscus?
(*Pause.*) Come on, Hogbin. I'm Blair. We've met. A couple of
years ago up in Blackheath, don't you remember?

HOGBIN: I'm afraid not.

BLAIR: Two days and nights in the back of a laundry van watching a
dead-letter drop for a pigeon who never turned up . . . I'll
never forget Blackheath.

HOGBIN: (*Carefully*) I *was* in Blackheath once.

BLAIR: Of course you were. That was you in the white apron,
brought me chicken in a basket. I mean a laundry basket. So
stop fooling about. (*Pause.*) Gladioli? (*Pause.*) All right, I'll
just sit on this bench and enjoy the view. The view north from
St James's Park is utterly astonishing, I always think. Domes
and cupolas, strange pinnacles and spires. A distant prospect
of St Petersburg, one imagines . . . Where does it all go when
one is in the middle of it, standing in Trafalgar Square with
Englishness on every side? Monumental Albion, giving credit
where credit is due to some sketchbook of a Grand Tour, but
all as English as a 49 bus.

HOGBIN: With or without chips?

BLAIR: As I remember it was a baked potato in silver foil, and a
KitKat.

HOGBIN: Hydrangeas.

BLAIR: That was it. I prefer Hydrangeas myself.

13

HOGBIN: I'm sorry, sir, but . . .

BLAIR: Perfectly all right. Keen gardener, are you?

HOGBIN: Do you run a man called Purvis, Mr Blair?

BLAIR: Rupert Purvis?

HOGBIN: Yes. He tried to kill himself last night. He killed a dog instead.

BLAIR: I see.

HOGBIN: Sir?

BLAIR: I said—I see.

HOGBIN: Oh. Well. Well, he jumped off Chelsea Bridge at 3.16 this morning, precisely at high tide. A precise man, Mr Purvis.

BLAIR: Yes.

HOGBIN: Unfortunately he landed on a barge.

BLAIR: You mean fortunately.

HOGBIN: I was looking at it from his point of view.

BLAIR: Of course.

HOGBIN: In fact he landed on a barge dog. The dog broke Purvis's fall. Purvis broke the dog's back. The barge dropped Purvis off downstream at St Thomas's.

BLAIR: And that's where he is now?

HOGBIN: Yes, sir.

BLAIR: Well, I'll pop down and see him. Thank you, Hogbin.

HOGBIN: There is something else, sir.

BLAIR: Yes. What kind of dog was it?

HOGBIN: I don't know, sir.

BLAIR: Well, it wouldn't be anything special. Fifty pounds, more than ample, wouldn't you say?

HOGBIN: I hadn't really thought, sir.

BLAIR: I would say fifty. If your Chief won't wear it, I dare say mine will.

HOGBIN: I didn't want to mention this to your Chief.

BLAIR: Oh, he's all right for fifty, don't worry. You worry too much, Hogbin, if I may say so. I'm grateful to you for taking this trouble but it would have been quite all right for you to come to the office.

HOGBIN: No, sir. I thought it was better to talk outside. It's not about the dog, sir. It's about a letter. Purvis posted a letter a few minutes before he jumped. We retrieved it.

BLAIR: You've been following him, Hogbin.

HOGBIN: We didn't know he was one of our own.

BLAIR: He wasn't yours, he was mine. Still is.

HOGBIN: That's what I meant.

BLAIR: Well, who did you think he was?

HOGBIN: We thought he was one of theirs.

BLAIR: I see.

HOGBIN: He was followed from Highgate Hill to a house in Church Street, Chelsea.

BLAIR: He lives there.

HOGBIN: Yes, so I gather. He left the house again just before three, leaving all the lights on. He knew he wouldn't have to pay any more bills. He walked to the river.

BLAIR: Posting a letter on the way. Whereabouts in Highgate did you follow him from? Highgate Hill Square?

HOGBIN: You obviously know all about it.

BLAIR: Everybody knows their safe house. Red Square we call it.

HOGBIN: We call it Dunkremlin.

BLAIR: Why?

HOGBIN: Sir?

BLAIR: Why did you follow him? Was he acting suspiciously?

HOGBIN: Not exactly suspiciously. He walked out of the front door, slamming it behind him.

BLAIR: Well, I give him a pretty free rein. When did you realize he was Q6?

HOGBIN: It was the letter. Here you are, sir. You understand, sir, that we had to open all the letters in the box in order to ascertain . . .

BLAIR: Yes, of course. Thank you. I'll read it later. Anything else?

HOGBIN: Sir?

BLAIR: I said—anything else?

HOGBIN: Well, the letter's a bit . . . Would you say that Mr Purvis had been overworking lately?

BLAIR: Well, *I* haven't been overworking him. But of course I can't speak for *them*.

Interior. Hospital.

BLAIR: Well, Purvis, this is all very silly. What on earth did you
think you were doing jumping off bridges?

PURVIS: Oh, hello, sir. How good of you to come.

BLAIR: Not at all. Are you quite comfortable?

PURVIS: Yes, thank you. I'm grateful for the private room.

BLAIR: I meant with your feet winched up like that. You put me in
mind of a saucy postcard.

PURVIS: I put the nurses in mind of midwifery. But I appreciate
your not mincing words. You're the first person who has
mentioned the word jump or bridge since I got here. I thought
I must have imagined it all. By the way, was there something
about a dog?

BLAIR: Yes. You're the first person to jump off a bridge on to a dog.
The reverse one often used to see at the Saturday morning
cinema, of course.

PURVIS: Men jumping off dogs on to . . . ?

BLAIR: No, dogs jumping off bridges on to . . .

PURVIS: Oh yes. What a relief anyway. I was beginning to think I'd
gone cuckoo.

BLAIR: Your relief may be premature. There's nothing cuckoo
about imagining things. Cuckoo is jumping off bridges. Are
you in any sort of trouble?

PURVIS: Well, one had a bit of a *crise*, you know.

BLAIR: Yes. Do you remember writing me a letter?

PURVIS: Have you received it already?

BLAIR: Special delivery.

PURVIS: I wasn't going to mention it.

BLAIR: I shouldn't have done so.

PURVIS: A bit of a shaker, I expect.

BLAIR: Well, these things happen in all families.

PURVIS: You mean that business about your wife. I'm sorry. It's the
last thing one would have expected of a woman who runs a
donkey sanctuary—concubine to an opium addict.

BLAIR: (*Huffily*) Now look here, Purvis—

PURVIS: Yes, I'm so sorry—one loses all one's social graces when
one expected to be dead.

BLAIR: I didn't mean *my* family. I meant Q6. People having what you call a bit of a *crise*. I suggest we draw the veil, eh? Least said, soonest mended.

PURVIS: You must do as you think fit. Personally I think you'd make an excellent number one, but I can quite see that you might take the view that it's nobody's business what the Chief gets up to in his own time so long as he doesn't bring his pipe to the office. Perhaps you think I'm a bit of a cad for sneaking?

BLAIR: These decisions are never easy. By the way, where did this story come from?

PURVIS: It's all over Highgate.

BLAIR: I see.

PURVIS: I was up there last night actually.

BLAIR: Really?

PURVIS: I went to visit my friend.

BLAIR: Oh yes?

PURVIS: He was none too pleased.

BLAIR: No?

PURVIS: I was after some information.

BLAIR: And did you get it?

PURVIS: No. I said to him, look, I said, can you just remind me— what is the essential thing we're supposed to be in it for?—the ideological nub of the matter? Is it power to the workers; is it the means of production, distribution and exchange; is it each according to his needs; is it the expropriation of the expropriators? Know what he said? Historical inevitability! Historical inevitability! You're joking, I said. Pull the other one, it's got bells on. No, you'll have to do better than that. Something can't be good just because it's *inevitable*. It may be good and it may be inevitable, but that's no *reason*, it may be *rotten* and inevitable. He couldn't see it. So I left. None the wiser. Perhaps you could help me on this one, Blair.

BLAIR: Oh . . . I don't know . . . they did give us a run-down on it years ago . . . one of those know-thy-enemy lectures . . . I didn't take much notice. There was something called the value of labour capital which seemed to be important but I never understood what it was.

PURVIS: No, I mean from your side of the fence.

BLAIR: Mine?

PURVIS: Yes. It's important to me. Can you remind me, what was the gist of it?—the moral and intellectual foundation of Western society in a nutshell.

BLAIR: I'm sorry, my mind's gone blank.

PURVIS: Come on—democracy . . . free elections, free expression, free market forces . . .

BLAIR: Oh yes, that was it.

PURVIS: Yes, but how did we deal with the argument that all this freedom merely benefits the people who already have the edge? I mean, freedom of expression advantages the articulate . . . Do you see?

BLAIR: You're going a bit fast for me, Purvis. I never really got beyond us being British and them being atheists and Communists. There's no arguing with that, is there? Are you quite sure you aren't in any sort of trouble?

PURVIS: Depends what you mean by trouble.

BLAIR: Your letter mentioned some unsavoury business with choirboys.

PURVIS: *Savoury* business, not unsavoury business.

BLAIR: Savoury business?

PURVIS: Yes. You know what a savoury is. Mushrooms on toast . . . sardines . . . or, in this case, Welsh rarebit.

BLAIR: I see. Well, you just have a jolly good rest, Rupert, take the weight off your feet . . .

PURVIS: As you see . . .

BLAIR: Yes, of course. But we'll soon have you back on them. You were lucky.

PURVIS: Luckier than the dog.

BLAIR: Yes. It was the dog that died.

SCENE 4

Exterior. Garden.

BLAIR: I admit it looks odd. The question is does it look odd enough?

SLACK: It looks odd enough to me, sir.

BLAIR: I'm not convinced, Mr Slack. I *do* like the mullioned window between the Doric columns—that has a quality of coy desperation, like a spinster gatecrashing a costume ball in a flowered frock . . . and the pyramid on the portico is sheer dumb insolence. All well and good. I think it's the Gothic tower that disappoints. It isn't quite *there*. It's Gothic but not Gothick with a 'k'. Should we ruin one of the buttresses?

SLACK: Ruin it, sir?

BLAIR: Mm . . . Make it a bit of a ruin. Or should we wait for the ivy to catch up?

SLACK: I should wait for the ivy, sir. We're going to have our hands full with the obelisk. Is it all right to lower away?

BLAIR: Yes, lower away.

SLACK: (*Calls out*) Lower away!

BLAIR: The crane has to swing it over slightly to the right.

SLACK: No, sir, it's centred on top of the tower.

BLAIR: But it's lop-sided.

SLACK: Only from where we're standing.

BLAIR: But surely, Mr Slack, if it's centred on top of the tower, it should look centred from everywhere.

SLACK: That would be all right with a round Norman tower, sir, but with your octagonal Gothic tower the angles of the parapet throw the middle out.

BLAIR: Throw the middle out—?

SLACK: The obelisk will look centred from the terrace, sir.

BLAIR: But it has to look centred from my study window as well.

SLACK: Can't be done now—you'd have had to have one side of the tower squared up with the window.

BLAIR: Hold everything.

SLACK: (*Shouts*) Hold everything!

BLAIR: This obviously needs the superior intelligence of Mrs B. I'll go and fetch her from the paddock.

SLACK: She's in the drawing room, sir.

BLAIR: I thought she was operating on one of the donkeys.

SLACK: That's right, sir.

SCENE 5

Interior.
Modest donkey noises.

BLAIR: (*Entering*) Pamela . . .
   (*The donkey brays and kicks the floor.*)
PAMELA: Hang on, Mrs Ryan.
BLAIR: I say, do be careful of my clocks.
   (*The room is going tick-tock rather a lot.*)
PAMELA: You've come just at the right moment. Mrs Ryan, you're
   doing very well but I can't do the stitches if there's so much
   movement.
MRS RYAN: Right-ho, dear.
PAMELA: Giles, you hang on to her legs.
BLAIR: I haven't really got time for all this.
PAMELA: Not Mrs Ryan's legs, Giles, Empy's.
BLAIR: Sorry.
PAMELA: There, there, Empy. Soon be over.
BLAIR: Look, Pamela, the donkey sanctuary is supposed to be the
   paddock. The drawing rooom is supposed to be sanctuary *from*
   the donkeys.
PAMELA: This is the only fire lit today and I needed it to sterilize the
   instrument. Hold her neck, Mrs Ryan.
MRS RYAN: Right-ho, dear.
PAMELA: Poor Empy got into a fight with Don Juan. It's only a
   couple of stitches . . . here we go, everybody . . .
   (*Silence, except for the ticking and tocking. Then the donkey brays
   and kicks.*)
BLAIR: For God's sake—she nearly kicked over my American
   Townsend.
PAMELA: Well, hold her *still*.
   (*Tense silence, marked by an orchestra of ticks and tocks.*)
   How long have I got before they all go off?
BLAIR: About a minute.
PAMELA: I don't see why they have to be *going* all the time.
BLAIR: If they weren't going they wouldn't be clocks, they'd be
   bric-à-brac. The long delay in the invention of the clock was
   all to do with the hands going round. If the hands didn't have

to go round, the Greeks could have had miniature Parthenons on their mantelshelves with clock faces stuck into the pediments permanently showing ten past two or eight thirty-five . . .

MRS RYAN: Were you expecting a clock today, sir? A package came for you, special delivery, sender's name Purvis.

BLAIR: Oh yes. Do you remember Purvis, Pamela?

PAMELA: Don't talk to me while I'm stitching. Isn't Empy being brave? Good girl.

BLAIR: I introduced you to him at the Chief's Christmas drinks. You said there was something funny about him. Pretty sharp. He tried to kill himself the other night. He killed a dog instead. He's sent me a family heirloom. I suppose I'll have to send it back now.

PAMELA: That must be what the note from Security was about. They opened your parcel in transit. They thought it was suspicious.

BLAIR: No, no I know all about it. Purvis has sent me an old sea captain's wooden peg-leg.

PAMELA: No he hasn't, he's sent you a stuffed parrot.

BLAIR: That's what I meant. There's one just like it on the piano in the trophy room at Cork Castle. That reminds me, there's a serious problem with the obelisk on the tower. It's going to look lop-sided depending on where one is standing, even though it's in the middle.

PAMELA: That's because of the corners. You should have had a round tower.

BLAIR: Why didn't you tell me?

PAMELA: I didn't think it mattered. The whole thing is fairly loopy anyway.

BLAIR: It's the old story—never change anything that works! I had in mind the obelisk at Plumpton Magna where they have a round tower but I thought I would go octagonal. It's entirely my own fault.

PAMELA: You mean your own folly. Can you reach the forceps?

BLAIR: Where are they?

PAMELA: On the grate.

BLAIR: Right.

(BLAIR *yelps as he drops the forceps. He yelps louder as the donkey kicks him. The donkey brays. All the clocks starts to chime and strike. The donkey gallops across the wooden floor and then out of earshot.*)

She kicked me!

PAMELA: I know just how she felt.

BLAIR: Well, the forceps were red hot.

(*The clocks are still going strong.*)

MRS RYAN: Is it all right if I get on now, dear?

PAMELA: Yes, all right, Mrs Ryan. Good job the french windows were open.

(MRS RYAN *switches on a vacuum cleaner.*

PAMELA *fades out calling for Empy as she leaves the room.*)

MRS RYAN: Can you lift your leg, dear?

BLAIR: No, I can't. The knee is swelling visibly.

MRS RYAN: Don't you worry, dear. I'll vacuum round you.

(*The clocks continue to strike.*)

SCENE 6

Exterior.   City park (St James's).   Day.
Big Ben is striking.

BLAIR: Good morning. I see the tulips are fighting fit.

HOGBIN: There's no need for that, sir.

BLAIR: No, no, just a passing remark. I thought you were keen on the things. Anyway, what's up?

HOGBIN: You remember that letter Purvis wrote you?

BLAIR: Yes?

HOGBIN: It's been on my mind.

BLAIR: You really *do* worry too much.

HOGBIN: Didn't it worry you, Mr Blair?

BLAIR: Well, some of it of course . . . but every family has occasional problems.

HOGBIN: You mean about Mrs Blair?

BLAIR: No, I don't mean anything of the sort. I really don't understand how some people's minds work. I was talking about Q6. We're a small department with, I like to think, a family feeling, and we have occasional problems, that's all.

HOGBIN: I'm sorry. I didn't believe a word of it, of course. The

22

whole letter was raving mad. I never read anything so obviously off its trolley. That's what worries me about it, as a matter of fact. That's why it's on my mind.

BLAIR: What do you mean, Hogbin?

HOGBIN: Well, sir—the opium den in Eaton Square, the belly dancer at Buckingham Palace, the sea captain's piano leg—

BLAIR: Parrot—it was a stuffed parrot.

HOGBIN: Well, whatever. And some scandal with an entire male-voice choir.

BLAIR: I asked Purvis about that. He said it involved a Welsh rarebit.

HOGBIN: You see what I mean.

BLAIR: No.

HOGBIN: I think the letter smells. I think he overdid it. I think he's shamming, Mr Blair.

BLAIR: Shamming what?

HOGBIN: I think Purvis *wanted* you to think he'd gone off his trolley.

BLAIR: But Hogbin . . . he did jump off Chelsea Bridge.

HOGBIN: At high tide. The absolute top. To the minute.

BLAIR: Exactly.

HOGBIN: When there was the shortest possible distance to fall.

BLAIR: Everybody goes too fast for me nowadays.

HOGBIN: Think about it, sir. There he is in the Soviet safe house in Highgate. What he's doing there I leave an open question for the minute. He makes a conspicuous departure, practically begging to be followed. He walks all the way home just to make it easy. He comes out flashing a letter which he posts, and then off to the bridge and over he goes—just as a handy barge is there to pick him up.

BLAIR: But he landed *on* the barge.

HOGBIN: It went slightly wrong. Especially for the dog.

BLAIR: You're not serious?

HOGBIN: No, I'm not. It's just not on. Apart from anything else the bargee and his family have been scudding about the river for three generations, real Tories, can't abide foreigners, wouldn't even eat the food. So that one is a non-starter. I'm just showing that the facts would fit more than one set of possibilities. There's something wrong with that letter. I know there is. You wouldn't like to tell me what Purvis was doing up in Highgate?

BLAIR: He was discussing political theory.

HOGBIN: I suppose you people know what you're doing.

BLAIR: Well, one tries.

HOGBIN: Where is Purvis now?

BLAIR: Convalescing. We maintain a house on the Norfolk coast, as a rest-home for those of our people who . . . need a rest. Sea breezes, simple exercise, plain food, TV lounge, own grounds, wash-basins in every room . . . It's like an hotel, one of those appalling English hotels. So I'm told—I've never been there.

HOGBIN: A rest-home for people who crack up?

BLAIR: You could put it like that. Or you could say it's a health farm.

HOGBIN: A funny farm?

BLAIR: I think that's about as much as I can help you, Hogbin.

HOGBIN: How is Purvis now?

BLAIR: I'm going to go and see him in a day or two. I'll let you know how I find him.

HOGBIN: *If* you find him. Is there a gate to this place?

BLAIR: No, as far as I know Purvis could make a dash for it in his wheelchair any time he chooses.

HOGBIN: I'm sorry if I seem to be obstinate. But there is something funny about that letter, sir. I don't know what it is.

BLAIR: Well, I'm afraid I must be getting back.

HOGBIN: Thank you for coming out to meet me . . . You seem to have been in the wars.

BLAIR: Got kicked on the kneecap, nothing serious. Goodbye— careful with my hand, burned my fingers . . . Oh, how I love this view!—what a skyline! All the way up Whitehall from Parliament Square, Trafalgar Square, St James's . . . It's like one enormous folly.

SCENE 7

Exterior.   Car arriving on gravel.   Motor mower at work in background.
The car draws up and comes to a halt. The car door opens and slams.
ARLON *is an old buffer who is mowing the lawn not far off.*

ARLON: Ahoy there!

BLAIR: Er—good afternoon.

ARLON: (*Approaching*) Spanking day!

BLAIR: Yes, indeed. Where would I find . . . ?

ARLON: Quite a swell.

BLAIR: Thank you.

ARLON: Force three, south-sou'-west, running before the wind all the way down from London, just the ticket.

BLAIR: Where would I find Dr Sed—?

ARLON: Hang on, let me turn this thing off.
(*The engine of the mower is cut to idling speed.*)
That's better. Welcome aboard.

BLAIR: I don't want to interrupt your mowing.

ARLON: Glad of the excuse to heave to, been tacking up and down all morning.

BLAIR: You're doing an excellent job here.

ARLON: Good of you to say so.

BLAIR: Deeply satisfying, I should think.

ARLON: Well, it's not everybody's idea of fun, running a bin for a couple of dozen assorted nervous wrecks and loonies, but I suppose it's better than cleaning spittoons in the fo'c'sle— even when London won't give us the money to pay a proper gardener. Still, there we are—you must be Blair. What happened to your fingers? Ice in the rigging?

BLAIR: How do you do? I'm sorry, I didn't realize . . . You are the warden here?

ARLON: I prefer the term keeper, just as I prefer the term loony. Let's call things by their proper name, eh?

BLAIR: Yes . . . Dr Seddon, isn't it?

ARLON: Commodore.

BLAIR: Commodore Seddon?

ARLON: You've come about Purvis, the scourge of the tidal bestiary, the one-man mission to keep the inland waterways dog-free, correct?

BLAIR: Well, yes.

ARLON: These secret service types, once they crack they can't stop babbling. Are you a member of the Naval and Military Club?

BLAIR: I don't recall.

ARLON: I used to be. But after certain words exchanged between myself and a brother officer in the card room it was not possible for me to remain. I said to the secretary—look chum, I said, the Arlons have been gentlefolk in Middlesex for five generations. We kept our own carriage when Twickenham was a hamlet and the Greenslades were as dust under our wheels, and I will not be called a jumped-up suburban card-sharp by a man whose grandfather bought a baronetcy from the proceeds of an ointment claiming to enlarge the female breast—a spurious claim moreover as an old shipmate of mine, now unhappily gone to her Maker, might have attested. Her Maker having made her the shape of an up-ended punt. Wouldn't you have done the same—?

BLAIR: I . . .

ARLON: I know you would. As far as that nine of hearts was concerned I accept that salting it away behind one's braces for a rainy day does not fall within the rules of Grand National Whist as the game is understood on land, I accept that without reservation, but certain words were uttered and cannot be unuttered, they are utterly and unutterably uttered, Blair, and if you want to do a chap a favour the next time you find yourself in Pall Mall, I'd like you to take out your service revolver and go straight up to Greenslade and—

BLAIR: Absolutely. Consider it done.

ARLON: Thank you, Blair. I shall sleep easier.

BLAIR: Don't mention it. By the way, do you happen to know where I might find Dr Seddon?

MATRON: (*Approaching across the gravel*) Good afternoon!

ARLON: I expect Matron will know. Say nothing about this. Take in a couple of reefs and batten the hatches.

BLAIR: Thank you very much.

MATRON: Mr Blair?

BLAIR: Good afternoon.

MATRON: Thank you, Commodore—please continue with the mowing.

ARLON: I don't take orders from you, you're just a figure-head and I've seen better ones on the sharp end of a dredger.

MATRON: Now, Commodore, do you want your rum ration with your cocoa or don't you?

ARLON: If I mow the lawn it is because it pleases me to do so.
    (*The mowing continues.*)
MATRON: Welcome to Clifftops, Mr Blair. I saw you talking to the
    Commodore from the window. He's one of our more difficult
    guests. I do hope it wasn't too awkward for you.
BLAIR: It's all right. He caught me on the wrong foot for a moment.
MATRON: You'll be wanting Dr Seddon. Let's go inside.
BLAIR: Thank you.
    (*They walk a few yards of gravel and then they are in interior.*)
MATRON: He's probably looking in on the ping-pong players in the
    library.
BLAIR: Ping-pong in the library? Isn't that rather disturbing?
MATRON: I suppose it is but most of them are already rather
    disturbed when they get here. See that one over there? He's
    dangerous. Let me take your coat.
BLAIR: I haven't got a coat.
MATRON: Never mind—in here—quick!
    (BLAIR *is pushed through a door which then closes.*)
BLAIR: What—?
MATRON: Sssh.
BLAIR: (*Whispering*) Where are we?
MATRON: In the coat cupboard. We haven't got long so don't waste
    a minute.
BLAIR: Really, Matron . . .
MATRON: Don't Matron me, I blew your cover the moment you
    showed your limp. I'm match fit and ready to go—parachute,
    midget submarine, you name it. The last show wasn't my
    fault, the maps were out of date.
BLAIR: Will you please open the—
    (*The door is opened.*)
SEDDON: Who is in there?
BLAIR: Ah, good afternoon— I'm looking for Dr Seddon.
MATRON: (*Sweetly*) And this, of course, is the coat cupboard.
BLAIR: Awfully nice.
SEDDON: Thank you, Bilderbeck. You may leave our visitor to me
    now.
MATRON: Matron to you, if you don't mind.
SEDDON: Have you had your tablets?
MATRON: (*Receding*) Mind your own business.

SEDDON: That's Bilderbeck. She used to dress up as a matron to oblige a chap she got mixed up with in Washington. When she was confronted with the photographs she insisted that she was giving him first aid and she's been sticking to her story ever since. It's the only uniform we allow here. We found that they tended to set people off. So we're all in civvies. Not even a white coat, as you see. You must be Blair. I'm Dr Seddon.

BLAIR: How do you do. Giles Blair. Look, don't take this amiss but would you have any form of identification?

SEDDON: First sensible remark I've heard today, counting the ones by the staff. Let's go to my office and have a cup of tea.

BLAIR: Thanks very much.

SEDDON: This way. How are things in London?

BLAIR: Relatively sane.

SEDDON: I know what you mean. My time with the firm was excellent preparation for Clifftops.

BLAIR: Oh . . . were you—?

SEDDON: Q10.

BLAIR: Code-breaking?

SEDDON: Code-*making*. You may have heard of consonantal transposition. Scramble your own telephone. That was my contribution to the fun and games.

BLAIR: Really? No, I . . .

SEDDON: We go up these stairs now. Yes, they never took it up. Said it was too difficult, or too simple, one or the other.

BLAIR: How did it work?

SEDDON: Posetransing stantocons, titeg?

BLAIR: Sorry?

SEDDON: Transposing consonants—get it?

BLAIR: (*Faintly*) Ingenious.

SEDDON: The trick was that there were no rules as such. You had to do it like improvising music. It just needed a little tackpris but cos fork the cuffing ditios dookn't tag the feng tif of.

BLAIR: What?

SEDDON: Moo yee sot I wean; tackpris! Well too yot, Blair . . .

BLAIR: Yot?

SEDDON: You see—pick it up in no time! Come up to the belfry, I've got something up there which will interest you.

28

BLAIR: What?

SEDDON: Bats.

BLAIR: Bats in the belfry?

SEDDON: Had them for years without knowing it. I say, not that
way . . .

BLAIR: Excuse me—I've got to find someone.

(BLAIR *starts hurrying back down the stairs.*)

SEDDON: Blair—?

BLAIR: Terribly sorry—I really have to go.

(*He gallops down the stairs. We go with him.*)

SEDDON: (*Distantly*) Blair . . . !

(*At the bottom of the stairs there is a collision.*)

BLAIR: I'm terribly sorry!

PURVIS: Blair!

BLAIR: Purvis! Thank goodness.

PURVIS: I'm very glad to see you.

BLAIR: I'm not sorry to see *you*. I'm damned if I can flush out
anyone in authority. Where's the chap who's supposed to be
running this show?

PURVIS: You mean Dr Seddon? I'll see if I can raise him for you.

BLAIR: Just as a courtesy . . . It was you I came to see, of course.

PURVIS: Really? That's awfully nice of you. I was about to have my
constitutional. Care to accompany me?

BLAIR: Glad to give you a shove. Front door?

PURVIS: Can't do the steps. This way is better.

BLAIR: How do you feel?

PURVIS: Like a mermaid on wheels. Did I hurt your leg?

BLAIR: That wasn't you. Burnt my fingers pulling Pamela's
chestnuts out of the fire, nearly knocked my Hilderson lantern
clock off the mantel and got kicked by the donkey for my
pains.

PURVIS: I'm awfully grateful to you for coming. It's impossible to
have a sensible conversation with anyone in this place.

(*They move to the exterior, garden.*)

There's a path through the rhododendrons to a view of the sea.

BLAIR: Tip me off if we run into Seddon.

PURVIS: He's probably up in the bell tower collecting guano for the
rose-beds.

BLAIR: Quite a decent clock up there. Reminds me a little of St Giles's in Cambridge. If it's a turret movement, I'd like to have a look at it. Did you say guano?

PURVIS: Yes. Seddon discovered a colony of bats up there the other day.

BLAIR: Bats in the belfry? Oh dear.

PURVIS: What's up?

BLAIR: Perhaps it would be better if I didn't see him. I'll drop him a note.

PURVIS: This is my favourite path. You can follow the top of the cliffs all the way round nearly to Cromer. At least you could if it wasn't for the wheelchair because of the boundary fence. Whoa!

BLAIR: Sorry.

PURVIS: Don't worry, this thing has got brakes. I don't come down this far if I'm on my own.

BLAIR: It *is* rather dangerous.

PURVIS: Not that. It's just a question of getting back up. You need strong wrists. There's a little flat bit to the side here, you could sit on that stump.

BLAIR: Fine. This is very pleasant. Do you mind if I pollute the atmosphere?

(BLAIR *lights his pipe and sucks on it.*)

Which way are we looking?

PURVIS: About north-east. That's the Dogger Bank out there, over the horizon a bit . . . the scene of the last occasion on which the Russian battle fleet engaged the British.

BLAIR: Really? When was that?

PURVIS: Ages ago. The Russian navy fired on some British trawlers.

BLAIR: Why?

PURVIS: It was a mistake. They thought the trawlers were Japanese torpedo boats.

BLAIR: In the North Sea?

PURVIS: As I said it was a mistake. I think it was a bit foggy, too.

BLAIR: It must have been.

PURVIS: It damned nearly led to war.

BLAIR: I should think it did.

PURVIS: The Tsar had to apologize to the King.

30

BLAIR: Oh . . .

PURVIS: Different Russia, of course.

BLAIR: (*Regretfully*) Yes, indeed.

PURVIS: They're getting there slowly.

BLAIR: Sorry?

PURVIS: Two steps forward, one and a half back. Narrowing the gap between rich and poor. That's what it's all about.

BLAIR: What?

PURVIS: Money, wealth.

BLAIR: I thought it was about freedom.

PURVIS: That's a luxury which has to be paid for. That's why the rich have always had it.

BLAIR: There's nothing in English law about what a man is worth.

PURVIS: There doesn't have to be. People only desire the freedom that is within their imagination. When you limit their horizon economically you limit their imagination. That's why the proletariat need the intellectuals—the failure of the masses to act is a failure of the mass imagination.

BLAIR: Purvis, what are you doing?

PURVIS: Just trying it out. How does it sound?

BLAIR: Like balderdash.

PURVIS: Really?

BLAIR: Doesn't it sound like balderdash to you?

PURVIS: Sometimes it does, sometimes it doesn't. That's my problem.

BLAIR: Well, we knew you had a problem, Purvis. What exactly is it?

PURVIS: Blair . . . you know how it is when you telephone someone and say, shall we meet at the Savoy Grill or Simpson's, and he says, I don't mind, make it Simpson's if you like, or do you prefer the Savoy, and you say no, that's fine, eight thirty suit you?, and he says fine, eight thirty, and you hang up—and *suddenly* you think—did he say Simpson's or the Savoy? It's gone, you know. You've lost it. Well, that's what's happened to me.

BLAIR: The Savoy or Simpson's?

PURVIS: No, it isn't *really* like that, except that when you try to

remember back, both ways sound equally right. I'm going
back thirty-five years now, when I was still being run by
Gell, or Rashnikov. Now Gell is dead and Rashnikov is
probably dead too. They set me going between them like one
of those canisters in a department store, and they
disappeared leaving me to go back and forth, back and forth,
a canister between us and you, or us and them.

BLAIR: I didn't quite follow that last bit.

PURVIS: I remember some of it, no problem. I remember striking
up a conversation with Rashnikov in one of the stacks in the
Westminster Library—political economy. Or perhaps he
struck up a conversation with me. I remember having a few
dinners with him, meeting some of his friends, arguing long
into the night about politics, and I remember finally being
asked to look something up for him in our back-numbers
room in Whitehall . . . You remember that basement we
used to have before we had microfilm? The thing he wanted
was perfectly innocuous, but by that time, of course, I knew
he was supposedly on the staff of the Soviet Commercial
Attaché, so the next time he asked me to look something up,
something which wasn't quite so innocuous, I of course
reported the whole thing to Gell who was my superior.

BLAIR: Of course.

PURVIS: Sure enough, Gell told me to pretend to swallow the bait
and to await instructions.

BLAIR: Straightforward enough.

PURVIS: It wasn't. Rashnikov was playing a subtle game. He had
told me to tell Gell.

BLAIR: To tell him what?

PURVIS: To tell Gell that I was being recruited by Rashnikov. So
that Gell would be fooled into thinking that I was pretending
to be Rashnikov's man while I was really Gell's man.

BLAIR: Looking at it from Rashnikov's point of view.

PURVIS: Yes.

BLAIR: And did you tell Gell that this was going on, that
Rashnikov had told you to tell Gell?

PURVIS: Yes. I did. But . . .

BLAIR: But . . . ?

PURVIS: Well, I'm pretty sure that when I told Gell that all
this was going on, I was also acting on Rashnikov's
instructions.
(*Pause.*)
BLAIR: But, if that were so, no doubt you told Gell that it *was* so.
No doubt you told Gell that Rashnikov had told you to tell
Gell that Rashnikov had told you to tell him that you were
being offered the bait.
PURVIS: That's what I can't remember. I've forgotten who is my
primary employer and who my secondary. For years I've
been feeding stuff in both directions, following my
instructions from either side, having been instructed to do so
by the other, and since each side wanted the other side to
believe that I was working for *it*, both sides were often giving
me genuine stuff to pass on to the other side . . . so the side I
was actually working for became . . . well, a matter of
opinion really . . . it got lost.
(*Pause.*)
Blair?
BLAIR: I didn't speak.
PURVIS: Well, I just carried on doing what I was told . . . and one
day, not very long ago, I started thinking about my
retirement. The sherry party with the Chief. The
presentation clock. The London Transport senior citizen's
bus pass. The little dacha on the Vistula.
BLAIR: Purvis . . . ?
PURVIS: Exactly. Hang on a sec, I thought—hello!—which—?
. . . ? And blow me, I found I had forgotten.
BLAIR: But you worked for Gell. For *me*.
PURVIS: I worked for Rashnikov too.
BLAIR: Only because we asked you to play along.
PURVIS: *He* asked me to play along.
BLAIR: Let's not get into that again. You're one of us.
PURVIS: Well, I'd have to be, wouldn't I, to be of any use to him.
BLAIR: You're a church warden.
PURVIS: I thought about that but if one were covering up would
one join a left-wing book club instead, for instance?
Obviously not. Well, I suppose one might as a double bluff.

Or, then again, one might not, as a triple bluff. I don't think I'm going to get to the bottom of this, to my infinite regress, I mean regret.

BLAIR: This is nonsense.

PURVIS: Rashnikov said to me once, you've got to believe in the lie so strongly that even if you confessed they wouldn't believe you. Or was that Gell? One of the two.

BLAIR: All you've got to do is remember what you believed.

PURVIS: I remember I was very idealistic in those days, a real prig about Western decadence. On the other hand I was very patriotic and really didn't much care for foreigners. Obviously one scruple overcame the other, but as to whether it was the Savoy or Simpson's . . . At some point it must have ceased to matter to me. That's what I find so depressing. Did they tell you I was depressed? It's on my file here: Purvis is extremely depressed.

BLAIR: My dear chap . . .

PURVIS: Well, it *is* extremely depressing to find that one has turned into a canister. A hollow man. Like one of those Russian dolls—how appropriate! Yes, I'm like one of those sets of wooden dolls which fit into one another as they get smaller. Somewhere deep inside is the last doll, the only one which isn't hollow. At least, I suppose there is. There used to be. Perhaps I'm not even a set of dolls any more, perhaps I'm an onion. My idealism and my patriotism, folded on each other, have been peeled away leaving nothing in the middle except the lingering smell of onion.

BLAIR: Please don't cry.

PURVIS: I'm sorry. It's the onion. Oh stuff it, Blair!

BLAIR: That's the spirit. To the taxidermist with the lot of it.
(*Sniffles and pause.*)

PURVIS: Did you get the parrot by the way?

BLAIR: Oh yes. I'll let you have it back, of course.

PURVIS: I'd like you to keep it. Find a place for it in your folly.

BLAIR: Most kind of you. Well, I ought to be getting back.

PURVIS: Thank you for coming.

BLAIR: Let me give you a push up the hill.

PURVIS: No, I'll stay here for a while. I'll manage. I like looking at the sea.

BLAIR: As for that other matter . . . You never told Rashnikov
anything which Gell hadn't told you to tell him, did you?

PURVIS: I never *knew* anything which Gell hadn't told me.

BLAIR: Well, there you are.

PURVIS: And I never knew anything to tell Gell which Rashnikov
hadn't told me.

BLAIR: So the whole thing is rather academic, isn't it?

PURVIS: Thank you for understanding, Blair.

BLAIR: Cheerio, then.

PURVIS: Goodbye, Blair.

SCENE 8

Interior.   Funeral service.
A choir.   Then BLAIR *and* HOGBIN *conversing under the singing.*

BLAIR: I thought I might find you here, Hogbin. Still worrying?

HOGBIN: Yes, sir.

BLAIR: Too late to worry now.

HOGBIN: Too late for Purvis, you mean.

BLAIR: Yes, poor Purvis. We were all at fault, especially me.

HOGBIN: Why?

BLAIR: Well, one asks oneself . . . with the benefit of hindsight,
was Clifftops the ideal place to put a man who had a tendency
to fling himself from a great height into a watery grave. Of
course, one didn't realize it was a tendency, one thought it
was a one-off, but even so . . .

HOGBIN: You think he jumped?

BLAIR: (*Sighs.*) What now?

HOGBIN: Just asking.

BLAIR: He wheeled. He rolled.

HOGBIN: Has anyone thought of checking the brakes on that
wheelchair, sir?

BLAIR: The wheelchair has not surfaced, Hogbin. Can you think of
anyone who required Purvis's death, or even stood to gain by it?

HOGBIN: He had friends in High . . .

(*The organ drowns him momentarily.*)

BLAIR: High places?

HOGBIN: Highgate. But then one would need to know more about
that than I'm allowed to know. I don't know anything. I don't
know what I'm doing here.

35

BLAIR: You're checking out the mourners. That's what you're doing here, Hogbin. You smell a mystery. You're looking for a lead. And as is often the case after sudden death, a good place to start looking is the funeral. Any interesting mourners? Anybody unusual? Unexpected? Anybody who looks wrong? Too aloof? Too engaged? Too glamorous?

HOGBIN: I spotted her. Any idea who she is?

BLAIR: None. Have you spotted Hoskins?

HOGBIN: Hoskins?

BLAIR: Third from the end with the eyelashes.

SCENE 9

Exterior. Churchyard.
The VICAR *is saying goodbye to the mourners.*

VICAR: Goodbye . . . goodbye . . . sad occasion . . . would have been so pleased . . . goodbye . . . goodbye . . .

HOGBIN: Thank you, reverend. A beautiful service. The choristers in glorious voice . . .

VICAR: Thank you . . . Mr . . . ?

HOGBIN: Hogbin.

VICAR: I noticed you at the back of the church, with the other gentleman. Were you colleagues of Mr Purvis's?

HOGBIN: Mr Blair is representing the firm. I was following in Purvis's footsteps. Perhaps I could walk along with you for a moment?

VICAR: I'm only going to the vicarage. We can take the side gate. We weren't quite sure what exactly Mr Purvis was doing.

HOGBIN: Quite. Incidentally, that lady in the red dress with the fingernails . . .

VICAR: She lodged with Mr Purvis in Church Street. Quite innocently, of course. One has to make the point nowadays, on the rare occasions when one is able to make it. I only met her once, a Turkish lady. She's a ballet dancer.

HOGBIN: Did you say ballet dancer or belly dancer?

VICAR: Ballet dancer. At least, I assumed she said ballet dancer. But now I come to think of it she does seem rather the wrong shape, and when I asked her where she danced she said Rotherhithe. Do you think she might possibly be a belly dancer?

HOGBIN: I'd put money on it. Let me hold the gate for you.

VICAR: Would you care for a spot of cheese?

HOGBIN: Thank you very much.

SCENE 10

Interior.

VICAR: Try this one, Mr Hogbin. This is a Caerphilly.

HOGBIN: (*With mouth full*) Welsh? I was going to ask you—

VICAR: Hardly any Caerphilly made in Wales any more—mostly in
    Somerset. A hundred years ago every farmhouse in that part of
    South Wales made its own cheese. A hundred and fifty years
    ago—what do you think?

HOGBIN: I don't know.

VICAR: It wasn't made at all! It's a newcomer, invented for the
    miners, makes an ideal meal underground, doesn't dry up,
    very digestible, and you can make it in two or three hours
    using hardly more than its own weight in milk. A Cheddar
    needs ten times its own weight in milk.

HOGBIN: I like toasted cheese. Welsh rarebit. Incidentally, Purvis
    mentioned—

VICAR: Now your cheese for Welsh rarebit is red Leicester. It'll
    never be so fine as a Cheshire because it doesn't go on
    maturing the same way, it's ready at three months, good for
    nine, finished at a year. But it's the best English cheese for
    melting. The orange colour is a tint, of course—carrot juice
    originally, but since the eighteenth century tinted with
    annatto, an extract from the *Bixa orellana* tree from the West
    Indies. You need one dram to every two and a half gallons of
    milk.

HOGBIN: Amazing.

VICAR: I'm always glad to meet a man who appreciates cheese.

HOGBIN: Did Purvis appreciate cheese . . . on toast perhaps?

VICAR: One doesn't like to speak ill of the dead, but I tell you now
    that Purvis may have liked the odd piece of cheese but he knew
    nothing about it, nothing at all. Purvis was a man who would
    melt an Epoisses on a slice of Mother's Pride as soon as look at
    you.

HOGBIN: An Epoisses?

37

VICAR: Purvis blamed the choir, but I'm not convinced. You would have really liked my Epoisses. I brought it back from Dijon. I chose one which had been renneted with fennel. The curd is milled, salted and then refined on rye straw. As soon as the mould starts forming the cheese is soaked in Marc de Bourgogne, an eau-de-vie distilled from local grape pulp. A beautiful thing, brick red on the outside, of course.

HOGBIN: Of course.

VICAR: I put it in the vestry because it can't abide central heating. That was a Wednesday.

HOGBIN: Don't tell me Purvis . . . ?

VICAR: Cut a great wedge out of it. The electric grill was still warm. I held up Matins for ten minutes while I searched the vestry for evidence.

HOGBIN: Did you find any?

VICAR: A half-eaten rarebit in Purvis's hymn book.

HOGBIN: An unsavoury business.

SCENE 11

Interior.

BLAIR's *chiming and striking clocks signal one o'clock. They require a spread of several seconds between them.*

PAMELA: Come and sit down, Giles. Soup's getting cold.

(BLAIR *grunts.*)

Are you going back to the office after lunch?

BLAIR: I suppose so.

PAMELA: Your funeral seems to have got you down.

BLAIR: It wasn't exactly *my* funeral.

PAMELA: Well, don't stand there brooding and looking out at the rain. What's worrying you?

BLAIR: Just thinking . . . I could have had a rustic pagoda.

(*A late clock strikes the hour.*)

The Graham bracket isn't itself, it's sickening for something. I'm pretty sure I know what it is. I'll have a look at it at the weekend. I think I've run out of copper sheeting . . . if I write down what I need could you pick some up for me from that place in Pimlico?

PAMELA: Must I?

BLAIR: It would be quite convenient for you, if you are in the vicinity, it's practically next door to Eaton Square.

PAMELA: Proximity and convenience aren't necessarily the same thing. Well, I'll try to fit it in.

(*Doorbell.*)

Are you expecting someone?

BLAIR: Half expecting. I'll go and see.

(*He goes through a door.*)

Don't worry Mrs Ryan, I'll get it!

(*He opens the front door.*)

Come in, Hogbin.

HOGBIN: I'm sorry to . . .

BLAIR: It's all right, I was half expecting you.

HOGBIN: Only half?

BLAIR: I was half expecting you to come here and half expecting you to telephone me to meet you in the park.

(*He closes the door.*)

Come in.

HOGBIN: Thank you, sir.

(BLAIR *closes a second door.*)

BLAIR: An interesting little funeral.

HOGBIN: Yes. I hardly know where to begin.

BLAIR: You talked to the vicar, of course.

HOGBIN: Yes.

BLAIR: A parochial scandal, as scandals go. I don't think for a moment that Purvis was guilty.

HOGBIN: Of what, exactly, Mr Blair?

BLAIR: Purvis wasn't your left-wing book-club type who would do down his vicar.

HOGBIN: What type was Purvis?

BLAIR: I would say he was loyal.

HOGBIN: Did you know he had an invitation to Buckingham Palace? To a garden party?

BLAIR: Yes. As a matter of fact I rather put it his way. The Department was due for one and, speaking for myself, I don't get much of a thrill any more from queueing up for a cup of tea and a fancy cake.

HOGBIN: He was going to take his lodger. She was most

disappointed that the invitation was not transferable.

BLAIR: The belly dancer?

HOGBIN: Exactly. I said there was something funny about Purvis's letter. And that's what it was—it's all true.

BLAIR: Well, of course.

(*Door opens.*)

PAMELA: Giles—

BLAIR: Darling, this is Mr Hogbin, a policeman. My wife, Pamela . . .

HOGBIN: (*Overcome with embarrassment*) Oh . . . how do you do . . . Mrs Blair . . .

PAMELA: How do you do, Mr Hogbin—please sit down.

HOGBIN: Thank you—oh! Sorry! I'm *terribly* sorry! I sat on your parrot.

PAMELA: It's not as bad as it looks, he was already dead. Giles, do remove him. I've given up on lunch. I'm off to see Don Juan—he hasn't been getting his oats. See you later perhaps, Mr Hogbin.

(*She leaves, closing the door.*)

BLAIR: You were saying.

HOGBIN: Yes. I'm awfully sorry.

BLAIR: What about? Oh, I see, yes. Would you like to give me the parrot? Thank you.

HOGBIN: Look, sir, if everything in Purvis's letter is true . . .

BLAIR: Oh, it's true all right.

HOGBIN: It's a situation. A bit of a bombshell.

BLAIR: Oh, come now. What sort of fool do you take me for?

HOGBIN: You mean you knew it was true?

BLAIR: Of course. One mustn't get over-dramatic about these things. One must try to be civilized about them. Keep them in the family.

HOGBIN: But surely, sir . . . the head of Q6 . . . an opium den in his own house . . .

BLAIR: Oh, *that*. That's a different matter. On that subject I would be inclined to say . . . that one mustn't get over-dramatic about these things.

HOGBIN: Over-dramatic? I don't see how one can be over-dramatic. You asked me a few days ago who might want

Purvis out of the way. It looks as if the answer is your Chief.

BLAIR: Why? I don't follow.

HOGBIN: An opium den in Eaton Square?!

BLAIR: Hogbin, you're in danger of making yourself look foolish. Too many tuppenny dreadfuls in your childhood reading. You and Purvis. A shiver of delicious horror runs right through your Farnham Royal morality. Opium den! The quintessence of moral depravity combined with dubious foreign habits. The Chief stoned to the eyeballs in a brocade dressing-gown, beating a gong when he is ready for the other half. Look, I've been in his den. TV, hi-fi, books, writing desk, dead animals poking their heads out of the wall, Axminster on the floor. It's not an opium den, it's a *den*. And to him, enjoying an occasional pipe would be simply a souvenir of a Far Eastern posting. Something brought home in the baggage like a carved ivory elephant. It isn't some ghastly secret for which you drive all the way to Cromer in order to tamper with the brakes of a wheelchair. You really are absurd, Hogbin.

HOGBIN: Are you trying to tell me to forget all about it?

BLAIR: Certainly not. You must make your report and give it to your Chief.

HOGBIN: That's what I intend to do. Mr Wren may have a different attitude.

BLAIR: I doubt it. In any case, if I were you I wouldn't bother Mr Wren with your murder theory.

HOGBIN: Why?

BLAIR: Because I had another farewell letter from Purvis.

SCENE 12

Purvis letter.

PURVIS: Dear Blair. Well, goodbye again, assuming that I don't fall into a fishing boat. Please don't feel badly. Suicide is no more than a trick played on the calendar. You may like to know that whether or not I left the fold all those years ago when my intellect aspired to rule my actions, I found at the end that my remaining affinity was with the English character, a curious bloom which at Clifftops merely appears in its overblown form. Looking around at the people I've rubbed up against, I see that with the significant exception of my friend in Highgate they all inhabit a sort of Clifftops catchment area; if we lowered our entry qualifications we would be inundated. I find this reassuring. I realize I am where I belong, at last, even though, in common with all the other inmates, I have the impression that I am here by mistake while understanding perfectly why everybody else should be here. In this respect Clifftops has an effect precisely opposite to being in a Marxist discussion group. I'm grateful to you for our chat. It led me to think about Gell and the way he used to wear hunting pink to the office in the season, and the way he used to complain about not being able to eat asparagus without dripping the butter after the first time he broke his neck, and I thought I *couldn't* have lied to Gell, not to Gell, not for a mere conviction. The man was so much himself that one would have been betraying him instead of the system. I hope I'm right, though I would settle for *knowing* that I'm wrong. Oddly enough, my friend from Highgate came to visit me, or rather to meet me at the boundary of the fence, and he tells me that the reason Rashnikov disappeared was that he had been recalled under suspicion of having been duped by Gell and me. Rashnikov said there was a logical reason why this should have been the impression given, but unfortunately he died of a brainstorm while trying to work it out. You might say that the same happened to me. My regards to your good lady. Yours sincerely, Rupert Purvis.

SCENE 13

Interior.
A cosy atmosphere. All three men, the CHIEF, WREN *and* BLAIR *are smoking pipes.*
BLAIR: There is something else, sir.
CHIEF: Yes. This dog. Now let's be reasonable about this, Wren. Quite unexpectedly the bargee has sent in a bill for three hundred pounds, claiming that his wretched dog was a

member of the Kennel Club and runner up in his class in the South of England Show. Is that correct, Blair?

BLAIR: Quite correct, sir, but . . .

WREN: I don't dispute any of that. I'm only saying that the dog was killed, in effect, by Q6, not by Q9.

CHIEF: We killed him but your man Hogbin filed the report confirming the dog's death as an incident during *his own case*. All the paper work is Q9, and, crucially, the bill for the dog was sent to Q9.

WREN: Look, I'm good for fifty if it helps. I'll put it in under dog-handling. I suppose Hogbin must have handled the dog.

CHIEF: Let's go halves. One-fifty each.

BLAIR: Excuse me, sir. Why can't we use Purvis's money? After all, he killed the dog.

CHIEF: Purvis's money?

BLAIR: Highgate kept giving him odd sums for film and bus fares, which we made him accept to preserve his credibility, and which Highgate made him declare for the same reason. There must be several hundred pounds by now, lying in some account somewhere.

CHIEF: Excellent. Well thought, Blair. Would you care for a pipe?

BLAIR: No thank you, sir. I'll stick to the old briar.

CHIEF: How is your pipe, Wren? Ready for another?

WREN: No thanks, it's bubbling along very nicely.

CHIEF: Jolly good. Well, that's that.

BLAIR: Actually it wasn't about the dog. It was about the opium. And your . . . your private life generally. Purvis said it was all over Highgate. I'd like to know how it got there.

CHIEF: Purvis took it up there. I put it into his Highgate package a couple of months ago. He was coming up for retirement and I thought that if they thought they had something on me I might get a tickle as his replacement . . . Nothing doing so far. Perhaps it's just as well. These double and triple bluffs can get to be a bit of a headache. It got to be a bit of a headache for Purvis.

WREN: How did it work?

(*The* CHIEF *speaks, slowly, deliberately, reflectively. The pauses filled with the gentle bubbling of his pipe.*)

CHIEF: Well, in the beginning the idea was that if they thought that we knew that they thought Purvis was their man . . . they would assume that the information we gave Purvis to give to them . . . would be information designed to *mislead* . . . so they would take that into account . . . and, thus, if we told Purvis to tell them that we were going to do something . . . they would draw the conclusion that we were *not* going to do it . . . but as we were on to that, we naturally were giving Purvis genuine information to give to them, knowing that they would be drawing the wrong conclusions from it . . . This is where it gets tricky . . . because if they kept drawing these wrong conclusions while the other thing kept happening . . . they would realize that we had got to Purvis first after all . . . So to keep Purvis in the game we would have to *not* do some of the things which Purvis told them we *would* be doing, even though our first reason for telling Purvis was that we did intend to do them . . . In other words . . . in order to keep fooling the Russians, we had to keep doing the opposite of what we really wanted to do . . . Now this is where it gets *extremely* tricky . . . Obviously we couldn't keep doing the opposite of what we wished to do simply to keep Purvis in the game . . . so we frequently had to give Purvis the wrong information from which the Russians would draw the right conclusion, which enabled us to do what we wished to do, although the Russians, thanks to Purvis, knew we were going to do it . . . In other words, Purvis was acting, in effect, as a genuine Russian spy in order to maintain his usefulness as a bogus Russian spy . . . The only reason why this wasn't entirely disastrous for us was that, of course, during the whole of this time, the Russians, believing us to believe that Purvis was in their confidence, had been giving Purvis information designed to mislead *us* . . . and in order to maintain Purvis's credibility they have been forced to do some of the things which they told Purvis they *would* do, although their first reason for telling him was that they didn't wish to do them.
(*Pause.*)
In other words, if Purvis's mother had got kicked by a horse

44

things would be more or less exactly as they are now.
(*Pause.*)
If I were Purvis I'd drown myself.

PURVIS: PS—Incidentally, Dr Seddon thinks that you ought to be in here yourself, but I'll leave you to field that one.

The Dissolution of Dominic Boot

A Play for Radio

Characters

DOMINIC
VIVIAN
TAXI DRIVER
SHEPTON
MOTHER
FATHER
GIRL CLERK
MAN CLERK
MISS BLIGH
CARTWRIGHT

Fade in street—traffic.

VIVIAN: Well, thanks for the lunch—oh golly, it's raining.

DOMINIC: Better run for it.

VIVIAN: Don't be silly . . . . (*Up*) Hey, taxi!

DOMINIC: I say, Viv . . .

VIVIAN: Come on, you can drop me off. (*To driver*) Just round the corner, Derby Street Library.

(*They get in—taxi drives.*)

DOMINIC: Look, Vivian, I haven't got . . .

VIVIAN: Dash it—that's taken about ten shillings out of my two-guinea hairdo—honestly, I'm furious. Don't you ever have an umbrella?

DOMINIC: Not when it's raining.

VIVIAN: Didn't I give you one for your birthday?

DOMINIC: No, it was your birthday.

VIVIAN: Why did I give it to you on *my* birthday?

DOMINIC: No, it was *I* who gave it to *you* on my birthday. *Your* birthday. Vivian, please stop talking about umbrellas. The thing is . . .

VIVIAN: If we're going out tonight, I'll have to have some repairs on my hair, it's beginning to straggle. Another pound down the drain.

DOMINIC: I'm afraid I can't tonight, Vivian, I promised to see my mother.

VIVIAN: What about?

DOMINIC: Um, about my father.

VIVIAN: What about him?

DOMINIC: Nothing. Just keeping her in touch.

VIVIAN: You never see your father.

DOMINIC: Well, we just sort of—talk about him.

VIVIAN: I thought you may be seeing her about us getting
married.

DOMINIC: Oh, no.

VIVIAN: What do you mean by that?

DOMINIC: I mean, yes.

VIVIAN: Will we have enough by Christmas, or spring at the
latest? After all, you've been saving now for months.

DOMINIC: Incidentally, Vivian . . .

VIVIAN: Oh, no! It's half-past two—Dominic, we'll have to start
eating somewhere with quicker service. Anyway, I'm fed up
with Italian. I don't know why we always go to Marcello's,
do you?

DOMINIC: No. Only . . .

VIVIAN: (*Up*) Just there, next lamppost on the right. (*Down*) By
the way, you're on the black list—you've had those six books
overdue for weeks—what do you do with them? (*Up*) Thank
you. (*Down*) Well, I'll see you tonight.
(*Opens door.*)

DOMINIC: I told you . . .

VIVIAN: Oh yes—tomorrow then, I'll see you in Marcello's.
Goodbye darling. Oh no, not Marcello's. Oh, I don't know—
phone me, will you?

DOMINIC: (*Slightly desperate*) Vivian—
(*She's gone.*)
(*Thinks:*) One and ninepence. Extras sixpence.
(*Coin counting:*) Sixpence, shilling, one and a penny, one
and two, three, threepence halfpenny . . . threepence
halfpenny . . .

DRIVER: Waiting till the rain stops?

DOMINIC: No, um, the Metropolitan Bank, Blackfriars, please.

Cut. Bank.

DOMINIC: In ones, please.

GIRL CLERK: Oh, Mr Boot, would you mind stepping down to the
end of the counter there . . .

DOMINIC: What for? Oh ah, righto. (*Humming.*)
(*Walking.*)
Hello, Mr Honeydew.

SHEPTON: I'm Mr Shepton.
DOMINIC: Oh really? I thought you were the manager.
SHEPTON: The manager is Mr Bartlett.
DOMINIC: Oh yes, I'm always getting it wrong.
SHEPTON: Well . . . yes, well, Mr Bartlett has asked me . . .
DOMINIC: Over the top, am I?
SHEPTON: You're forty-three pounds beyond your limit, Mr Boot.
  I'm afraid that we have had to pass back two cheques
  received today from ah Marsello's er Markello's . . .
DOMINIC: Marchello's, Mr Sheppard.
SHEPTON: Shepton.

Cut. Taxi moving.
DOMINIC: (*Thinks:*) Three and three . . . three and six . . .
DRIVER: The Irish Widows' International Bank—is that on the
  left here?
DOMINIC: No, other side. Thanks. (*Thinks:*) Three and six, plus
  six, four bob . . .

Cut. Bank.
DOMINIC: In ones, please.
CLERK: Oh, good afternoon, Mr Boot. Would you have a word
  with Mr Honeydew?

Cut. DOMINIC *slamming taxi door.*
DOMINIC: Co-operative Wool and Sythetic Trust Bank in High
  Street, Ken, please.
DRIVER: You a bank robber, are you?
DOMINIC: In a modest way. Please hurry, I've got to cash a cheque
  before they close.
  (*Taxi starts moving.*)

Cut to traffic.
DRIVER: I did my best.
DOMINIC: Dammit.
DRIVER: Six and nine.
DOMINIC: Ah, would you mind taking a cheque?

Cut. A door is flung open.

MISS BLIGH: (*Very remote, quite detached*) Good afternoon, Mr
 Boot. Mr Cartwright has been asking . . .

DOMINIC: In a minute—can you lend me ten bob—I've got a
 taxi . . .

MISS BLIGH: Oh Mr Boot, what a pity you didn't come earlier. I've
 just spent it all on stamps—five pounds' worth, Mr Boot.

DOMINIC: Hang on.

 (*Out door—cross pavement.*)

 I say, do you take stamps?

DRIVER: Yes, if you like. Green Stamps, are they?

DOMINIC: All colours. I mean they're stamps. I don't know what
 colour they are. *Stamps*!

DRIVER: Do you mean like for letters?

DOMINIC: That's right, and parcels. Stamps.

DRIVER: Do me a favour.

 (*Back across pavement through door.*)

DOMINIC: No good . . .

MISS BLIGH: Oh, what isn't, Mr Boot? Oh, you're terribly wet, is it
 raining?

 (DOMINIC *through another door.*)

DOMINIC: I'm sorry to trouble you, Mr Cartwright. . .

CARTWRIGHT: I've been waiting forty-five minutes to trouble you,
 Mr Boot. Now look here, I'm going out for the rest of the
 afternoon, but I want to pick up the Lexington figures to
 take home, so please have them ready by six. Well,
 look to it.

DOMINIC: Mr Cartwright—could you lend me ten shillings. . .

Cut to taxi moving.

DRIVER: Nice area. What number are you?

DOMINIC: Forty-eight. On the left.

DRIVER: You use taxis a lot, don't you?

DOMINIC: Yes, hardly ever. I mean no, I do . . . . (*thinks:*)
 Fourteen shillings . . . and six . . .
 (*Taxi pulls up.*)
 Thanks, I'll be out in a minute.

DOMINIC: (*Panting, muttering*) Fourteen and six, fourteen and six . . . property of the North Thames Gas Board . . . oh well . . . where's that poker . . . wardrobe, wardrobe—ah!—North Thames, here goes, uh . . . .
(*Breaks open gas meter—coins.*)
One, two four, five six seven, ten, ten and six, ten and six . . . oh no, damn . . . oh God . . . .

Cut. In taxi—moving.
DOMINIC: First left, second right. Oh, would you like ten bob to be going on with, here.
(*Coins.*)
DRIVER: You been robbing the gas meter?
DOMINIC: No, no, I just collect them. (*Thinks:*) Twenty-one and six—plus sixpence, minus ten bob I gave him, minus one and threepence halfpenny, that makes—twenty-two bob, plus sixpence, minus ten bob I gave him.
DRIVER: (*Pulling up*) Here we are, 73, Mansion Lane.
MOTHER: (*On pavement*) Taxi!
DOMINIC: Hello, Mother. I was just coming to see you.
MOTHER: Dominic! You always pick the wrong time. Never mind we can talk in the taxi. (*To driver*) Bond Street.
DOMINIC: Going shopping?
MOTHER: Hair-do. They always ruin it, but I don't trust anyone else. I'm thinking of going blue. And piled on top. Well, what's with Vivian?
DOMINIC: A bit straggly—the rain, you know.
MOTHER: What are you talking about? Why are you so wet? Don't you use Vivian's umbrella?
DOMINIC: No, why should I? She doesn't even use the one I gave her.
MOTHER: I mean the one she told me she gave you, for Christmas.
DOMINIC: (*Is everyone mad?*) She–never–gave–me–an–umbrella!
MOTHER: I like that girl. Have you seen anything of your father?
DOMINIC: No.
MOTHER: I'm told he's thinking of getting married again.
DOMINIC: Who'd have him?

MOTHER: God knows. I think you ought to go and see him. I think it's quite wrong not to keep in touch with one's father.

DOMINIC: Righto. (*Thinks:*) Twenty-four, minus ten, plus . . .

MOTHER: And if you find out anything about her, give me a ring at once. Why aren't you at the office?

DOMINIC: Well, things are a bit slack, and I'm my own boss now really, so I thought I'd take an hour off and have tea with you.

MOTHER: Well, it seems to be the first job you're any good at. I hope you're being sensible about it. I bet you're not saving.

DOMINIC: Oh, I am.

MOTHER: I was getting quite tired of you always coming to see me for money. Good God—twenty-five shillings—Dominic . . .

DOMINIC: (*Trapped*) It's all right—it's all on the office—I've been making some calls for them, you see, old Cartwright. . . . (*Thinks*) Oh God. . . .

Cut—DRIVER *driving*.

DRIVER: You know who used to cut my mum's hair? My dad.

DOMINIC: He was a hairdresser, was he?

DRIVER: No, he was a grocer. Corner shop off the Angel.

DOMINIC: (*Thinks:*) Thirty-one minus ten plus . . .

DRIVER: And guess who cut *his* hair. My mum.

DOMINIC: (*Thinks:*) Thirty-nine, and sixpence for Vivian and sixpence for Mother, minus ten, plus, no minus . . . . (*Up*) Can you lend me four pennies?

Cut—DOMINIC *dialling*—*phone*.

DOMINIC: (*On phone*) Hello, Charlie. Dom. Dominic. Is that Charles Monkton? Well, it's Dom. Dominic Boot. Yes—listen, Charles I'm in a bit of a fix—you know that two pounds I lent you? Yes, now. I'll come over. Where's your place? What? I'm not coming by train—I'm in a taxi. No, that's WHY I'm broke, Charlie—what? All right. Past East Croydon station, first left, 18B. Right.
(*Down phone.*)

Cut.

DRIVER: You ever been to Croydon?

DOMINIC: No, Why?

DRIVER: It's over the six-mile limit.

DOMINIC: Limit?

DRIVER: Yes. You see, if you stop me, then I've got to take you wherever you want, that's the law. But if it's over six miles the meter doesn't count so I'm allowed to fix a price. That's the system.

DOMINIC: That's ridiculous.

DRIVER: Well, I lose on tips, you see. I can take you there, well in that time I can have four other fares and a tip on each. So I'm allowed to strike a bargain with you. Two pounds.

DOMINIC: A pound.

DRIVER: Right, you can pay me off now.

DOMINIC: Twenty-five bob.

DRIVER: Doesn't pay.

DOMINIC: Thirty with tip.

DRIVER: Thirty-two and six.

DOMINIC: Done!

Cut. In taxi—stationary.

DOMINIC: (*Thinks:*) Seventy-one in all. Minus ten I gave him. Sixty-one. Three pounds one. One and threepence halfpenny in change. About three pounds, then. Minus two of Charlie's. One pound. Minus, minus nothing. One pound, one pound. Who? Please God, who? Plus fourpence he lent me. One pound and fourpence. *Who?*

DRIVER: Well have you made up your mind? Can't sit in Croydon for ever. There's a fellow there who's looking like mad for a taxi. Looks like a town fare. If you don't want to go, say so quick.

(*Door opens—*DOMINIC *in street.*)

DOMINIC: Excuse me, you seem to be rather desperate for a taxi.

MAN: I am—I've got an important meeting . . . why?

DOMINIC: I think I can help you. Please take my taxi.

MAN: How very kind of you. Are you sure?

DOMINIC: Certainly. I'm in the business.

MAN: Business?

DOMINIC: I'm a taxi agent. That'll be twenty-five shillings.

MAN: I'll call a policeman.

DOMINIC: Very well, one pound and fourpence, and you pay the tip.

Cut—DRIVER *driving*.

DRIVER: What did that copper want?

DOMINIC: Little misunderstanding. (*Thinks:*) A hundred and eight, minus ten, minus two pounds . . . (*Up*) You must make a fortune.

DRIVER: Shilling a mile I have to give the company for this cab. And there's my fuel. I'd never keep body and soul together without the shop.

DOMINIC: Grocer's?

DRIVER: Clothes, furniture, stuff, second-hand. I've got a staff. My brother. He cuts my hair. Well, my mum and dad have passed on.

Cut.

DOMINIC: Father! Oh dear Father who art in Windsor . . .

FATHER: Good Lord, what brings you here?

DOMINIC: Well, I was missing you, Father.

FATHER: Don't be absurd. Still, good to see you. How's your mother?

DOMINIC: Very well, Father. Sends you her love.

FATHER: Nonsense. For goodness' sake sit down. Whisky?

DOMINIC: Fine. Oh, Father, by the way—I've got a cab outside . . .

FATHER: Can't you even walk ten minutes from the station? You people. (*Up*) Bates! Give this half crown to the taxi driver and bring us some whisky. Well now, Dominic, how's the job?

Cut.

DRIVER: Who was that?

DOMINIC: My father.

DRIVER: He seemed angry about something.

DOMINIC: He'd just had some bad news. Derby Street Library,
please.

Cut.
DOMINIC: (*A desperate man*) Vivian!
VIVIAN: Ssssh . . . . (*Whispering*) For goodness' sake, what's the
matter?
DOMINIC: (*A desperate man whispering*) Oh sorry. I say Vivian . . .
VIVIAN: Have you brought the books at last?
DOMINIC: Books? Oh—look, Vivian, please help me, you get paid
today don't you? I've got to pay off that taxi, you see . . .
VIVIAN: Oh, Dominic—I'm very cross with you—we're saving to
get married and you keep taking taxis everywhere. It's not
fair, Dominic. Now you come running to me. Honestly.
DOMINIC: (*The desperate man, cracked and yelling*) OH, YOU STUPID
COW, SHUT UP AND GIVE ME TEN POUNDS FOR THE LOVE OF GOD!

Cut. Interior.
DRIVER: Well, frankly, you couldn't have paid much for it, could
you?
DOMINIC: It's a very fine engagement ring. Ten guineas.
DRIVER: See that? Scratched. Four pound ten.
DOMINIC: It's a diamond. Six pounds.
DRIVER: Five and I'm taking a chance.
DOMINIC: Done. What about the rest of the stuff?
DRIVER: Well it's a bit of a mess isn't it? I don't know how you
can live like this, I don't really. I mean, it's really junk, isn't
it? I'll give you ten bob for the desk, and another ten for the
mirror. The bed's had it really—I mean six books isn't the
same as a castor, is it? Thirty bob with the mattress. Now
over here. Not a bad wardrobe—fifteen bob—gas stove—
couple of pounds if you like. That's about it, isn't it? OK,
Dom? Look, someone's bust up your gas meter.
DOMINIC: What about the clothes? There's some good stuff there.
DRIVER: Can't move it, you see. I'll give you ten bob to take it
away, and that makes us square, doesn't it?
(*Doorbell.*)
Oh, that'll be my brother with the van.

DOMINIC: Mr Melon.

DRIVER: Lemon.

DOMINIC: Mr Lemon, I've got to get back to the office before six. You couldn't throw that in, could you?

DRIVER: Can't do it, Dom. Company checks the mileage, you see. That's a seven and a tanner drive, that is. Tell you what, I'll cut my throat and do it for the suit.

DOMINIC: What suit?

DRIVER: That one you got on.

DOMINIC: But that only leaves me with a pair of pyjamas and a raincoat. I can't go to the office like that. Can I?—*Can I?*

Cut. Door flung open.

DOMINIC: Is he back yet?

MISS BLIGH: Hello, Mr Boot. Is it still raining? Oh, you are wet. I do like your pyjamas Mr Boot. What's the matter Mr Boot, you seem awfully upset. Mr Cartwright seems upset too. (*Door opens.*)

CARTWRIGHT: Well, Mr Boot—Good God, man, what are you wearing? Have you gone mad?

DOMINIC: I don't think so, Mr Cartwright.

CARTWRIGHT: Get out of here. I'm giving you a week's notice. And stop crying.

DOMINIC: Yes, Mr Cartwright. (*Door slams.*)

MISS BLIGH: (*Always tender, soft, remote*) Come on, Mr Boot. I think you ought to go home. Come on . . . I'm going your way, Mr Boot.

DOMINIC: (*Weeping*) Oh . . . oh . . . (*They go through door into street.*)

MISS BLIGH: It's raining again. Haven't you got an umbrella, Mr Boot? Don't cry, Mr Boot. Your pyjamas are getting awfully wet . . . I should do up your front, Mr Boot, you'll catch cold. . . . Pull your socks up, Mr Boot. (*Up*) Taxi! . . . come on, Mr Boot. Come on, you can drop me off. . . .

'M' is for Moon Among Other Things

A Play for Radio

Characters

CONSTANCE
ALFRED

Silence—a man grunts and shakes his paper—a woman flips over the pages of a book and sighs.

NB A married couple, ALFRED *and* CONSTANCE—*middle class, childless, aged 45 and 42.*

CONSTANCE: (*Sighs—thinks:*) Macbeth . . .
  (*Flip.*)
  Macedonia . . .
  (*Flip.*)
  Machine-gun . . .
  (*Flip.*)
  Magna Carta . . .
  (*Flip.*)
  Measles . . .
  (*Flip.*)
  Molluscs . . . molluscs . . .

ALFRED: (*Grunts—thinks:*) ' . . . the girl, wearing a red skirt and black sweater, asked the court that her name should not be continued in column five, continued in column five . . . '
  (*Shakes paper.*)

CONSTANCE: (*Thinks:*) . . . Invertebrate animal . . . discovered that marine varieties . . .
  (*Slams book shut.*)
  I think enough for tonight—I wish the print wasn't so small . . . Have you seen my pills anywhere?

ALFRED: Mmmm . . . (*Thinks:*) ' . . . "anything like it in my thirty years on the Bench," he added. "While young louts like you are roaming the streets no girl is safe from . . . "'
  (*Impatiently*) Oh . . .
  (*Turns page.*)

CONSTANCE: (*Thinks:*) February the fifth, March the fifth, April, May, June, July, August . . . six.

ALFRED: (*Thinks:*) 'A Smooth-as-Silk Beauty as Fast as they Come!'

CONSTANCE: (*Thinks:*) The Friday before last must have been the twenty-seventh, that's right, because the Gilberts came to dinner and that was a Friday because of Mrs Gilbert not eating the meat, and the Encyclopaedia always comes on the twenty-seventh, and it was just when the M to N came when I phoned Alfred at the office about what to give the Gilberts, so it must have been Friday the twenty-seventh. So last Sunday was the twenty-ninth, so today is twenty-nine plus seven makes thirty-six, so it must be the sixth, unless July has thirty-one, in which case it's the seventh, no, the fifth. Thirty days hath April, June, is it? Wait a minute, the Friday before last was the twenty-seventh . . .

ALFRED: (*Thinks:*) 'I found her to be a smooth-as-silk beauty with the classic lines of thrust of . . . '

CONSTANCE: Alfred, is it the fifth or the sixth?

ALFRED: Mmm? (*Thinks:*) ' . . . surging to sixty mph in nine seconds . . . '

CONSTANCE: Fifth?

ALFRED: Fifth what?

CONSTANCE: What's today?

ALFRED: Sunday . . . (*Thinks:*) ' . . . the handbrake a touch stiff and I'd like to see an extra ashtray for the passenger but otherwise . . . ' (*Up*) Oh for goodness' sake—you know I hate people looking over my shoulder.
(*Turns page.*)

CONSTANCE: (*Thinks:*) August the fifth, nineteen sixty-two. (*Up*) Alfred, in half an hour I'll be exactly forty-two-and-a-half years old. That's a thought, isn't it?

ALFRED: Mmmm . . . (*Thinks:*) 'Little old grey-haired Mrs Winifred Garters wept last night as . . . '

CONSTANCE: What time were you born, Alfred?

ALFRED: What?

CONSTANCE: I was born just as the clock struck half-past ten at night—what time were you born?

ALFRED: I can't remember.

CONSTANCE: Didn't anyone tell you?

ALFRED: That's what I can't remember.

(*Hall clock chiming ten.*)

Oh, what's that?—ten? We haven't had the news today. I think there's one now, isn't there? Turn on the box—hang on, where's the *Radio Times*?—ah—is this this week's?

CONSTANCE: Forty-two-and-a-half, and all I've got is a headache.

ALFRED: Is this the new one? 'August five to twelve'—what's today?

CONSTANCE: Sunday.

ALFRED: No–no–no—what's—oh never mind—yes, this is it—News at five-past ten.

(*Turns on TV.*)

'Dial M for Murder'—oh, that might have been good.

CONSTANCE: It's an awful thing, you know. When you start worrying about the halves. I mean there's no purpose to make sense of it, is there? Every time it's half-past ten, it's another day older, and all I've done with it is to get up and stay up. Where's it all going?

(*Bring in finish of 'Dial M for Murder'—hold it and fade it low.*)

(*Thinks:*) They used to call me Millie . . . my middle name was my favourite till I was—how old was I? 17? Happy Birthday Millie, it used to be . . . Then I went over to Constance, it sounded more grown-up. Seventeen from forty-two. Twenty-five. A quarter of a century, constant Constance. . . . (*Up*) If I had a choice, perhaps I'd choose what I'm doing now. I don't care about that. But I want the choice. I don't want the moon, Alfred, all I want is the possibility of an alternative, so that I know I'm doing this because I want to instead of because there's nothing else.

ALFRED: Sshssh—hang on, Constance, let me hear the News . . .

(*Bring in opening of tape (if there is one) of the 10.05 pm News—5 August 1962.*)

NEWS: The News . . . Marilyn Monroe, the actress, was found dead in her Los Angeles home today . . .

(*Fade out.*)

ALFRED: (*Fading in with 'oh's' used as a sort of dirge—thinks:*)
Oh . . . oh . . . oh . . . oh . . . oh . . . poor Marilyn . . . poor poor thing . . . What have they

done? . . . God, poor little thing . . . She must have been so unhappy. Oh Marilyn . . .

CONSTANCE: She seemed so full of life, didn't she?

ALFRED: (*Thinks:*) Abandoned . . . no love . . . like a child . . .

CONSTANCE: Poor thing, it's awful.

ALFRED: (*Thinks:*) Marilyn . . . you shouldn't have trusted them, they're all rotten . . .

CONSTANCE: Do you suppose she meant it? Oh, wasn't she lovely, I mean a lovely *person*, she made you feel it. Doesn't it go to show?

ALFRED: Oh, do shut up.

CONSTANCE: Alfred!

ALFRED: Oh, I'm sorry. I'm just tired . . . and upset.

CONSTANCE: It's all right, Alfred.

ALFRED: Of course she meant it. By God, you've only got to use your imagination. It's such a cold shallow world she was living in. No warmth or understanding—no one understood her, she was friendless.

CONSTANCE: Do you think so?

ALFRED: Of course. Hangers-on. People didn't appreciate her. Just using her. A girl like that. It's a crime . . .

CONSTANCE: Fate.

ALFRED: Fate! Don't be absurd!

CONSTANCE: Please don't shout, Alfred.

ALFRED: (*Wearily*) Oh damn them, dammit . . . Oh, let's go to bed. I'm tired.

CONSTANCE: Yes. I'm worn out—hope I'll be able to sleep.

ALFRED: I can never stay awake, and you can never get to sleep—what's the matter with you?

CONSTANCE: I don't know—can't sleep with this headache.

ALFRED: You know, you read too much, you're always complaining of eye strain and headaches, well it's no wonder.

CONSTANCE: The print's too small, really.

(*Flip flip flip of pages:*)

ALFRED: The Universal Treasury of People, Places and Things: Illustrated. M to N . . . A lot of useless knowledge.

CONSTANCE: I've got as far as Molluscs, but I'm skipping madly.

ALFRED: You forget it all anyway.

64

CONSTANCE: No I don't, not all of it.

ALFRED: Well, you forgot about Catholics, didn't you? There must have been *something* about them under C.

CONSTANCE: (*Unhappy, offensive-defensive, a little desperate*) Oh Alfred, *please*—not now again . . .

ALFRED: *Catholics*! Catholics-don't-eat-meat-on-Fridays. Or under M—*Meat*!, what-Catholics-don't eat-on-a-Friday. Or F—*Friday*!, the-day-Catholics-don't-eat-meat-on. Oh my God, you could probably have found it under G—*Mrs Gilbert*!, wife to Alfred's boss *Mr* Gilbert and a staunch Catholic who does not eat meat on a Friday! (*Pause.*) D is for Débâcle—that which occurs when Mrs Gilbert is offered meat by her husband's chief accountant's wife on a Friday!

CONSTANCE: (*Crying*) Well, I wouldn't have forgotten if you hadn't been so awful on the phone—I phoned you to ask you what to get for dinner and you wouldn't give me a chance— Alfred—you were—you behaved . . .

ALFRED: Oh, don't cry—I couldn't talk to you then . . . You had to call up just as Mr Gilbert, Anglican, was hovering round my neck with my monthly report . . . Oh, what does it matter anyway . . .
(*Pages turned.*)
M is for Money . . . Universal Treasury all right . . . Two guineas a volume, a guinea per letter of the alphabet. How can you get a guinea's worth out of X? Or Z?

CONSTANCE: It was a lovely birthday present.

ALFRED: Well, I'm sorry I haven't got as much money as your rich brother Stanley.

CONSTANCE: Oh, you know I didn't mean that. But it's lovely to know that every month there's another volume coming. That's the seventh, counting the A to B I got on the actual day. It's O to P this month. Oranges and Orang-utans. I don't know—it's just that the time isn't all a waste, somehow, do you know what I mean?

ALFRED: What's the capital of Mongolia?

CONSTANCE: The point isn't to know the capital of Mongolia, Alfred—the point is to . . . Alfred, at half-past ten I'll be forty-two-and-a-half years old and it's all slipping by.

ALFRED: Well, I'm blessed—do you know they haven't even got *her* in here.

CONSTANCE: Who?

ALFRED: 'Monroe Doctrine . . . Monroe, James, President of the United States . . . ' Universal ruddy Treasury.

CONSTANCE: Well, they can't have everything. I remember my first ABC book—everything was so simple then. I thought that each letter only stood for the one word they gave, you know? A is for Apple, B is for Baby, C is for Cat . . . M was for Moon. It was ages before I knew that M was for anything else . . . like Millie . . . She was 36, he said, didn't he?

ALFRED: Did he? Poor dear . . . What I meant was that it needn't have happened. That's why you can't call it fate.

CONSTANCE: It's all right, I wasn't thinking.

ALFRED: It was just that she had no one to recognize her needs, you see. No one to turn to, I mean. No wonder the poor girl got desperate. Those *actors*—people like that—they've got no humanity, no understanding—self, self, it's such a selfish society. A girl like that, dying with a telephone in her hand— who did she have to call who would have done her any good? No one. Perhaps that's fate.

CONSTANCE: Yes, I suppose so.

ALFRED: Well, let's go up. I'll lock up—you have the bathroom first.

CONSTANCE: I wonder who she was trying to phone, though . . . (*Fade out—sound of* CONSTANCE *getting into bed—or near offer.*) Oooooh, bed. I feel quite worn out.

ALFRED: You got up too early again.

CONSTANCE: I couldn't drop off once I woke up. It's getting very tiresome.

ALFRED: Don't those pills work?

CONSTANCE: I suppose they must help. I think I'll take an extra one tonight.

ALFRED: Yes, I should.

CONSTANCE: Oh—Alfred—I forgot my glass of water. Do you mind, while you're still up.

ALFRED: Oh, gosh, where is it?

CONSTANCE: On the wash-stand. (*Thinks:*) Oh God, if I'd been in her place I would have eaten the bloody meat and gone to confession . . . Bitch . . . I shouldn't have phoned Alfred at the office, though . . .

ALFRED: Here you are. Got the pills?

(*Clock chiming half-past ten*—ALFRED *getting into bed.*)

CONSTANCE: (*Thinks:*) Half-past ten, August the fifth, nineteen sixty-two. Well—Cheers! (*Gulps pill and drink.*) Happy anniversary, Millie.

(*Puts glass down.*)

ALFRED: Should I turn the light off?

CONSTANCE: Yes.

(*Click.*)

(*Thinks:*) Maple tree, Mozambique . . . Mandragora . . . Marzipan . . . Mother . . . Moon . . . Melon . . . Menopause . . . Mongolia . . .

ALFRED: (*Thinks:*) Marilyn . . . don't worry, I'm glad you phoned, . . . Don't be unhappy, love, tell me all about it and I'm sure I'll think of something . . . Do you feel better already?—Well, it's nice to have someone you know you can count on any time, isn't it? . . . Don't cry, don't cry any more . . . I'll make it all right . . . (*Up*—*sigh*) Poor old thing . . .

CONSTANCE: Oh, you mustn't worry about me, Alfred, I'll be all right . . . (*Thinks:*) Marshmallow . . . Mickey Mouse . . . Marriage . . . Moravia . . . Mule . . . Market . . . Mumps . . .

Teeth

A Play for Television

Characters

GEORGE POLLOCK—early thirties, a saloon-bar Lothario,
handsome, big white smile.

HARRY DUNN—the dentist; smaller, middle thirties, very clean
and pink, light-framed spectacles; tight, even, white smile.

THE WIFE—30, white housecoat (dental receptionist), neat, hair in
bun, good teeth.

AGNES—young spinster, on the shelf, sad.

FLORA—a bit older, same boat.

The waiting room.
Tatty furniture, ancient magazines.
Three people.
AGNES *and* FLORA *sit together, conspiratorially, on a settee, speaking
quietly, on the borderline of audibility as far as* GEORGE POLLOCK *is
concerned. From behind his illustrated paper, he eavesdrops, his eyes
switching over the top of his paper. That is to say, we see the paper first
(it is* Woman's Own*) and then* GEORGE *peeps from behind it. We note,
now or later, that he has been studying a bra-and-panty ad. But* AGNES
is coming through now.

AGNES: The first thing I thought was—I'll have to kill myself now.
FLORA: No!
AGNES: Oh yes. I knew it was the end. And it was the real thing for
    me.
FLORA: He wasn't worth it.
AGNES: (*Sighs.*) I don't know. There never was another for me.
FLORA: Plenty of fish in the sea, I say.
AGNES: Different kettle altogether. Yes, I seriously considered it.
    That'll teach him, I thought.
FLORA: What'll?
AGNES: *Killing* myself.
FLORA: Ah. Serve him right.
AGNES: Yes, it would've. You'll be sorry, I thought, Jack
    Stevens—*then* you'll know. (*Sighs again.*) Yes, I came close; I
    wouldn't be here today if we hadn't been all-electric.
FLORA: (*Nods sympathetically.*) He was luckier than he knew.
AGNES: He would've carried his burden of guilt to his
    grave . . . instead of which he's got a very nice trading station
    in the China Seas. (*A reprise*) . . . You'll be sorry, Jack
    Stevens—then you'll know what you've done.

71

FLORA: What brought it about, then?

AGNES: (*Leans closer with meaningful intent.*) Walked into the bathroom without knocking.

FLORA: No!

AGNES: Without so much as a by your leave.

FLORA: Disgusting.

AGNES: Said he didn't know I was in there.

FLORA: Well, he would, wouldn't he?

AGNES: And he did.

FLORA: What did you do?

AGNES: Turned my back quick as a flash. But he'd seen.

FLORA: He knew what he was doing all right.

AGNES: '*Agnes*,' he said 'what have you done to your *teeth*?!' (*Pause.*)

FLORA: Teeth?

AGNES: I was brushing my teeth after dinner. It's only the two middle ones that come out—the rest's my own, what there is, but of course it's the *gap*, isn't it?

FLORA: Oh yes. It's the gap that'd give you away.

AGNES: (*Recalling it with tragic clarity*) '*Agnes*, . . . what have you done to your *teeth*?!' . . . It wasn't the same after that with Jack Stevens. A week later he'd got his third mate's papers and he was taken away, over the horizon, by a dirty black tramp—yeh Irene Castle from Cardiff, I still look out for her.

FLORA: Got all her own teeth, has she?

AGNES: 'sa boat.

(POLLOCK (*hereafter*, GEORGE) *has allowed his curiosity to leave him exposed, ear cocked, eavesdropping. The two women catch him at it. He gives them a great white smile.*

The door into the reception room opens. The receptionist (the WIFE) *does not notice* GEORGE *at first and seems about to summon one of the two women. But* GEORGE *has stood up. The* WIFE *is somewhat taken aback but recovers: she changes the summons.*)

WIFE: Er . . . Mr Pollock . . .

(*The women stare at the queue-jumper* GEORGE *as he follows the* WIFE, *smiling.*)

(*To the women*) Mr Dunn won't keep you a moment . . .

(GEORGE *and the* WIFE *go into the reception room. As soon as the door is closed behind them, the* WIFE *turns to him in urgent enquiry, keeping her voice down.*)
What's the matter?

GEORGE: Nothing—I mean—

WIFE: You shouldn't come here—
(*She glances at the second closed door which leads into the surgery.*)

GEORGE: Why not?

WIFE: I'm not impressed—just because you've got a guilty conscience—

GEORGE: No . . .

WIFE: Well, you should have—

GEORGE: I'm sorry, lover—I was terribly disappointed myself—really disappointed.

WIFE: And don't call me lover—

GEORGE: I'm sorry—(*tries to touch*—) Who gave you those earrings—?

WIFE: (*Moves away.*) You let me down—

GEORGE: I had to demonstrate a new line—there was big money involved—They (*earrings*) aren't real pearl, are they? Can't be—

WIFE: You've got another on the side—How many sides have you got?

GEORGE: Oh now, that's cynical, that is—

WIFE: Yesterday of all days—

GEORGE: Listen, you musn't be so possessive—who gave you those earrings?—

WIFE: A very good friend.

GEORGE: Don't give me that—you're a respectable married woman. It was Harry, was it?

WIFE: It was my birthday—

GEORGE: I know it was your birthday—I told you I couldn't get away.

WIFE: You can get away when it suits you—You're going off me—

GEORGE: How could I?—Think of last Saturday after tea—it doesn't add up—

73

WIFE: Lust—

GEORGE: Oh, I'm hurt—

WIFE: I knew it was a mistake—

GEORGE: Don't let's have regrets—

WIFE: Don't make me laugh—

GEORGE: Don't cry—

WIFE: You make me sick. I don't care anyway—I've been looking about, too, you know—

GEORGE: No, I bet it was Harry—Very nice, too—cultured, of course (*the earrings*)—

WIFE: Think you can get away with anything—*will you please stop grinning*!

GEORGE: Smiling—I've got a nice smile—Come here, you misguided sexy insatiable receptionist you—

(*He reaches to touch her: she recoils. Eyes on surgery door.*)

WIFE: For goodness' sake!

GEORGE: He can't hear us.

WIFE: Anyway, I'm working—

GEORGE: Live dangerously—let yourself go—

WIFE: Oh, give over—

GEORGE: You like my smile really—it's one of the two things you like about me—

WIFE: You're only like this when you're trying to make up—

GEORGE: We're friends again, aren't we?

WIFE: Are we?

GEORGE: Kiss and make up—

WIFE: Listen, you can't carry on like that here—

GEORGE: Don't worry about him—

WIFE: You've got to go now—you shouldn't have come—there are patients waiting—

GEORGE: I'm a patient—

WIFE: Please, George—they've got appointments—

GEORGE: I've got an appointment—

WIFE: You haven't—

GEORGE: Yes I have—

WIFE: What for?

GEORGE: Teeth.

WIFE: You've got toothache?

GEORGE: No, it's my check-up. Six-monthly.

WIFE: It's not. (*Going to her desk diary.*)

GEORGE: Yes it is—would you care to examine me?

WIFE: Oh, stop it, will you?—(*scanning the diary*) I can't find it—

GEORGE: There was a reminder at the office—

WIFE: What reminder?

GEORGE: My appointment. I can see the system's cracking up— you can't keep your mind on it, or off the other.

WIFE: I thought you came to see *me*—I thought you came to be nice—

GEORGE: I am being nice—I'm charming the pants off you— that's what brought us together.

(*He advances, she backs, glancing at the surgery door.*)

WIFE: You make me ashamed.

(*The surgery door opens; the* WIFE *jumps;* HARRY DUNN *smiles.*) Look who's here, Harry.

HARRY: Hello, George. Nice to see you.

GEORGE: How are you, Harry?

HARRY: Ready and waiting.

WIFE: I'm sorry—we were—

GEORGE: Having a natter.

HARRY: Right you are. Well, come on in. (*To the* WIFE) Tell you what—as it's George, while I'm just giving him the once over, could you carry on with the files—I'll give you a buzz if there's any concrete to be mixed.

GEORGE: You won't find much wrong with *my* choppers.

HARRY: (*To the* WIFE) In flashing form, is he?

GEORGE: Ooh, he's wicked, isn't he?

(*The* WIFE *smiles wanly. The two men go into the surgery,* HARRY *closing the door.* HARRY *has a full complement of dental apparatus. It is a good-sized surgery, and the chair and machine sit in a good space, silent, waiting, ready for* GEORGE. HARRY *and* GEORGE *look at it a moment, as though the apparatus were a third occupant.*) Well . . .

(*He goes to meet it. Sits in the chair. There is some little 'business' over the first few lines of dialogue: principally,* HARRY *is sorting and readying a few shiny metal implements, and he fixes the paper-towel bib round* GEORGE'*s neck.*

The machine is a modern one. Its body holds two or three
squirters, rather like the nozzle of a petrol pump, only the rubber
tube attached disappears into the machine when the nozzle is not
in use: plus a swivel table for the tools: and the big praying-mantis
leg of the high-speed drill.

HARRY *should make use of all his tools and nozzles, squirting air*
and water, swivelling, drilling, etc. The point is that as HARRY *is*
playing with GEORGE. *The dental procedure does not have to be*
authentic or accurate. The director and actors can assume that
there is nothing much wrong with GEORGE'*s teeth, and that there*
is a logical rationalization for using the machine indiscriminately
for effect.)

HARRY: Haven't seen you for a while.

GEORGE: No—you know how it is. I've hardly had time to turn
round.

HARRY: Hard at it, are you?

GEORGE: My life's not my own.

HARRY: Yes, I was only saying to Prudence—we haven't seen
George for ages.

GEORGE: Yes, we'll have to get together.

HARRY: Of course, we lead a very quiet life compared to yours, I
expect.

GEORGE: I'm never at home.

HARRY: Out and about, on the town—that's George all over—I
told Prudence.

GEORGE: On the job.

HARRY: Lovely work if you can get it. Mind you, we haven't had a
lot of chance anyway—with Prudence going to the evening
classes.

GEORGE: Oh yes.

HARRY: Did you know about that?

GEORGE: Er . . . no.

HARRY: Shows how long it is since we had you round. Now, let's
have a look at you.

(GEORGE *opens his mouth.* HARRY *peers and probes . . .*)

. . . Yes, there's her flower-arranging . . . dressmaking—I
don't know, she shouldn't be bored—I mean, she's a career
woman really—but she's got to fill up her life. And then

76

there's her charity work . . . did you know about her charity work?

GEORGE: (*Signifies denial*) Ughnugh.

HARRY: Must have been soon after we last saw you that she took it up. Helps with old people, once or twice a week, takes them about, cheers them up, poor things. She's more out than in . . . Still, it's only a matter of time till *I'm* an old person so I expect she'll have more time for me then . . . (*Smiles: withdraws.*)

(GEORGE *closes his mouth. Reaches for the mouthwash.*)

GEORGE: Well, mud in your eye, Harry—I see it's your round.

(GEORGE *washes out his mouth and sits back.*)

HARRY: No wonder she's so tired.

GEORGE: What?

HARRY: Prudence. Yes, I was only saying to her—it's about time we had George and Mary round for a game of cards. We used to enjoy that. Lovely girl, Mary—one of the best. Just as well she's a working wife, I suppose.

GEORGE: How do you mean?

HARRY: How's *your* social life?

GEORGE: Oh, very quiet.

HARRY: Quiet evenings at home.

GEORGE: That sort of thing. Only I'm never there. That's why they're quiet.

(*He starts to laugh, but has to open his mouth for* HARRY.)

HARRY: Yes, just as well for Mary—she's not the sort to sit around the house . . .

(*He probes.*)

You've been letting yourself go a bit, haven't you?

(GEORGE'*s worried eyes.*)

I'm glad you came in today—this is a serious warning, George; you think what people can't see isn't happening— but it all comes out in the end. Your sins always find you out.

(GEORGE'*s eyes:* HARRY *probes.*)

I can spot the signs you know, a mile off, so you better watch it, hadn't you? I must say, I wouldn't have thought it of you.

(*He withdraws long enough for*—)

GEORGE: Now hold on, Harry—

(HARRY *flicks on the spotlight. The glare is in* GEORGE's *eyes.*
GEORGE *grips the sides of the chair.*)

HARRY: I'm giving you fair warning—and Mary wouldn't thank
you for it if it came to the worst, would she?

GEORGE: Look here—

(HARRY *squirts.*)

HARRY: Gums—it's your gums you have to watch, they're the
ones doing it. You haven't been taking my advice—I told
you: daily massage and woodpoints in the crannies. If your
gums go then the lot goes. (*He withdraws.*) A serious
warning, George.

GEORGE: Oh—(*In relief he takes a swig of water.*)

HARRY: You're not supposed to *drink* it.

GEORGE: My teeth are fine, Harry—I mean I don't want to teach
you your job but—(*He has to open his mouth to say 'but' and in
goes the steel.*)

HARRY: No pain?—there?

(*Jab:* GEORGE *jumps.*)

Yes, I thought as much.

GEORGE: You caught my gum there, Harry—

(HARRY *sighs and turns away, fiddling with his tools.*)

HARRY: Ah well . . . Yes, I've given it a bit of thought and I'm
going to have it out.

GEORGE: What?

HARRY: I mean—she gets home absolutely dead beat. She just
wants to go to sleep.

GEORGE: Oh. Well, I suppose it takes it out of her.

HARRY: The flower-arranging?

GEORGE: Oh well, I suppose it requires a certain concentration.

HARRY: You may be right. *You*'ve got the best of it.

GEORGE: Me?

HARRY: Well, entertaining clients and that sort of thing—at least
you can take Mary along.

GEORGE: Oh, it's not her kind of thing. Business, you know. It's
just hard work.

HARRY: Same boat, then.

GEORGE: Yes.

HARRY: Of course, women notice these things.

GEORGE: What?

HARRY: When you get home dead beat. Just want to go straight to sleep.

GEORGE: Oh yes.

HARRY: Same thing with me and Prudence. Only the other way round, of course. Makes one very tense, you know—and in my job you've got to have a very steady hand, got to be cool and calm—

(*He turns round with a wicked tool.*)

GEORGE: Harry!—(*He brings his voice down.*) There's nothing wrong, is there Harry?

HARRY: Well, I've seen better, George. I don't know if I can save that one.

GEORGE: Don't be daft.

HARRY: Pink toothbrush—admit it.

GEORGE: What?

HARRY: They've been bleeding, when you brush your teeth.

GEORGE: Well, a bit, perhaps. Now and again.

HARRY: Pyorrhoea.

GEORGE: What?

HARRY: Setting in. (*Shakes his head.*) I've told you before, George—you've only got one set of teeth. Let them go once and they've gone for good. Now look at my teeth—(*he shows them*)—I wasn't born with better teeth than you, but I look after them. I massage the gums. Use woodpoints on them. I've got a row of good strong white shiny teeth for that. See? Teeth are very important on every level. I mean, apart from anything else, it was my teeth that first attracted Prudence to me—she told me that.

(GEORGE *starts to speak but* HARRY *is in there: jab.* GEORGE *winces.*)

There—see that? Blood.

(GEORGE *starts to protest, to move.*)

Hey—hold on, mouth open, head still—I don't want to slip with this little number.

(GEORGE *freezes in alarm.* HARRY *probes.* HARRY *starts to whistle softly.*)

. . . Yes, Prudence is very particular about teeth. I'm sure

Mary's the same. She's got a lovely smile herself . . . Of course, I'm not saying that teeth are a key to a man's *character*, but it's the smile women look for. (*He withdraws.*) I mean, that swine Collins had good teeth, I'll give him that, and he took Prudence in completely.

GEORGE: What?

HARRY: Oh—have I spoken out of turn? Well, it's all water under the bridge now.

GEORGE: What is?

HARRY: Collins—a trainee from the dental hospital. Nasty piece of work. Thought I was an idiot.

GEORGE: Oh?

HARRY: Well, you know what Prudence is—very impressionable, a bit young and dizzy, a sitting duck for a bastard like Collins—I wouldn't tell Mary about this, you know, women don't like each other to know when they've made a bit of a fool of themselves—but there was a little something between Prudence and Collins. Well, I didn't blame *her*, of course—I mean, she's an innocent, really—Collins took advantage of her. No, I just handled it my own way.

GEORGE: Really?

HARRY: Oh yes. Collins wouldn't be showing his face around the fair sex for quite a while to come . . . and a real smiler, he was. It was the craftiness I didn't like. He was seducing her right under my nose and he thought I couldn't see. An insult to my intelligence—that was it.

GEORGE: What did you—?

(HARRY *has turned round, holding a syringe.*)

What's that?

HARRY: No point in causing unnecessary suffering, is there? (GEORGE *opens his mouth to protest:* HARRY *says* 'That's it' *and puts in the needle.*) We'll just give it a minute . . . Yes well, I didn't go to law, if that's what you mean. I *could* have done— oh yes, an open and shut case—I could have sued him for thousands. But of course there was no point—I mean, he wasn't a man of substance. If he'd been a man of substance, I wouldn't have hesitated. Thousands. And the scandal. It would have ruined a man of substance. How's business?

GEORGE: What?

HARRY: Doing well? I always said to Prudence George is a man with a big future. Barring accidents. Oh yes.

GEORGE: Well, it's all go. No time to myself for weeks.

HARRY: Of course it is. How's the rowing?

GEORGE: The what?

HARRY: I thought you were a rowing man.

GEORGE: No, I wouldn't say that.

HARRY: Oh, I thought you were a great one for the sculls on the Serpentine.

GEORGE: Not me.

HARRY: Umm. Well . . . getting numb?

GEORGE: What? Oh—yes, I think so.

HARRY: Let's have a look. (*Probes* . . .) . . . Yes, funny business. I mean, I had no reason to disbelieve it, because I know that with Tuesday being Prudence's free afternoon—
(GEORGE *jerks*.)
Sorry!
(HARRY *withdraws*.)
Better leave it a minute, then. (*Sighs*.) Who can one believe then?

GEORGE: Oh—of course—I'm with you—you mean on the Serpentine with Prudence.

HARRY: That's right.

GEORGE: *Rowing*!

HARRY: That's what I said.

GEORGE: Yes—quite. I mean, it wasn't actually *rowing*.

HARRY: No?

GEORGE: No—it was more in the nature of paddling.

HARRY: Ah.

GEORGE: Yes, I was in the Park, and you don't often get a chance to have a bit of a paddle—yes, I was just fixing up a boat for myself—it was more a canoe, really—and lo!—there was Prudence—'Hello,' I said, 'What are you doing here?' 'Hello,' she said, 'fancy seeing you.' 'Fancy a paddle,' I said . . . Yes, she mentioned seeing me, did she?

HARRY: No, she didn't mention it. It was Archie Sullivan.

GEORGE: Who?

HARRY: Archie Sullivan. Do you know him?

GEORGE: No, I don't believe I do.

HARRY: Oh. He knows *you*.

GEORGE: Oh.

HARRY: Yes, he told me he saw you and Prudence having a bit of a row on the Serpentine on her afternoon off work. I can't think what she was doing in the Park—though of course she does have her activities as I told you.

GEORGE: Yes, it was the flowers, I think. Picking flowers. To arrange.

HARRY: That's funny.

GEORGE: Well, I suppose you have to bring your own—you won't find the local authorities lashing out the rates on floral composition.

HARRY: No, but Tuesday is old people.

GEORGE: Oh—yes—She did have some old people with her. Three or four. Very decent lot, I thought. Very clean and well behaved.

HARRY: Did you have them in the boat?

GEORGE: No, they didn't fancy it.

HARRY: Very nice.

GEORGE: What?

HARRY: Very nice, if you can get it. I don't know how you do it. Still getting your bit, then? On the job?

GEORGE: Now, Harry—

HARRY: No, I envy you—what a job! Lovely.

GEORGE: Oh, the job—Well, it's very varied work, of course—

HARRY: Yes, you should have been on 'What's My Line?'. They'd never have guessed you, would they, not with your mime. There you'd be rowing your boat—they'd never guess Salesman in a million years. You'd have got a diploma.

(*He has wandered off and has suddenly turned round with a mallet and chisel.* GEORGE *sits bolt upright and squawks—*)

GEORGE: Harry!

(HARRY *puts the chisel against the head-rest bracket and gives it a good thump with the mallet.*)

HARRY: Must get that seen to. (*He puts down the mallet and chisel.*) Open up now. (*Probes.*) Yes, you won't feel a thing.

(*The drill:* GEORGE's *eyes.*)

Mmmm . . . (*Whistles softly for a moment.*) Incidentally, when you and Mary come round could you bring Prudence's shoes with you.

(GEORGE's *eyes.*)

Steady now. (*Withdraws.*)

GEORGE: What?

HARRY: Apparently she left them at your place after she fell in.

GEORGE: What are you talking about?

HARRY: Shoes. She left them behind. At your place after she fell in. Of course, that's my deduction, I may be wrong.

GEORGE: You are wrong, George. What are you trying to say?— Prudence never came home without her shoes, did she?

HARRY: No, she was wearing Mary's. Lucky thing you live so close to the Park—she might have got pneumonia with her shoes wet.

GEORGE: Mary's shoes?

HARRY: Got Mary's name in them. Same kind of shoes, only with Mary's name in them. Lucky they take the same size. Must remember to thank her. Rinse please.

(GEORGE *rinses and thinks.*)

GEORGE: Oh—yes. Of course. Yes, it was when she was getting out of the boat, she sort of—

HARRY: Fell in.

GEORGE: Well, no—I mean—she certainly got her feet wet, yes. 'Tell you what,' I said—'My place is very handy—I'll just nip up for a pair of Mary's shoes for you to go home in, don't want to get pneumonia—'

HARRY: But she went with you, didn't she?

GEORGE: Well, it seemed simpler, yes—cup of tea to warm her up—footbath—Yes, you asked her about it, did you?

HARRY: No, I've hardly had a chance to speak to her. It was Archie Sullivan who told me.

GEORGE: Oh? I must say, he gets about doesn't he: (*Laugh.*) *He* ought to have been on 'What's My Line?' if anyone—with *his* mime—just following people about, they'd never guess him in a million years.

HARRY: Oh, I don't know. I mean, he's a private enquiry agent, isn't he?

GEORGE: Is he?

HARRY: Well, he says he is. I don't see why he should lie about it.
(*Up*) Mary!
(*The door opens and the* WIFE *enters.*)
Ah, Mary—this husband of yours is having a bit of trouble after all—

WIFE: Not serious is it, Harry?

GEORGE: I meant to tell you, lover—you'd never guess who I met in the Park—
(*He finds his mouth full of drill.*)

HARRY: (*Drilling*) Well, it's not too good at all. He hasn't been taking care. I'm trying to save what I can.
But . . . (*Withdraws.*)
(GEORGE *starts to speak.*)
Spit.
(GEORGE *rinses.*)

GEORGE: Yes—I couldn't get a taxi—traffic jams as far as you could see—and I had to meet this big client—so I thought, I know—I'll cut through the Park—and of course I forgot about the lake—bang in the way—so what do you think I did? I'll tell you—
(HARRY *has returned with brush and liquid.*)

HARRY: Now whatever you do, don't move your head while I'm doing this.

GEORGE: What does it do?

HARRY: Stains green—we don't want to get it on your teeth, but it's very good for your gum condition, so I'm giving it a try. Ready?
(GEORGE *freezes with mouth open.* HARRY *administers. The* WIFE *mixes paste.*)
. . . I was just saying, Mary—old George has a very interesting job. Takes him into all sorts of places.

WIFE: Mostly pubs.

HARRY: Yes—and the lake.

WIFE: What lake?

HARRY: The Serpentine. You'll never guess what he was doing yesterday.

WIFE: Demonstrating a new line, he said.

HARRY: Ha–ha—that's a new line—eh, George?

84

(GEORGE *frozen*.)

(MARY *comes round to the front and notices the extractors. She picks them up*.)

MARY: Harry, you don't mean—?

HARRY: Don't worry—you won't know the difference.

MARY: (*Upset*) It's not the same, though, is it?

HARRY: Well, he should have thought of that in all these months of neglect.

MARY: But he's always brushing his teeth. He's a maniac about them.

HARRY: It's the gums, Mary, it's the gums. Oh—you moved, George!

(*He withdraws*.)

Yes, he was on the lake, demonstrating—

GEORGE: Life-jackets. Have you got green on my teeth?

MARY: Life-jackets?

GEORGE: The new line. I was demonstrating it, rowing a boat— the client was worried about it causing restriction—He was going to order a thousand as long as it didn't interfere with the rowing—that's what he said—so I went out and—

MARY: Life-jackets. It was my birthday, too. He let me down, you know.

HARRY: Tsk, tsk. You don't know when you're well off, George— a beautiful wife—

MARY: Oh really, Harry—

HARRY: Beautiful, I said—and on her birthday—if I was in your shoes, George—oh, that reminds me—Ah!—you moved again? Where was I?

MARY: Do you think I'm beautiful, really, Harry?

HARRY: I say it in front of George. A man would be proud to have you for a wife.

MARY: Oh, Harry—isn't he sweet, George? You see I've got them on? (*Earrings*.)

HARRY: You do something for those earrings. They're nothing by themselves.

MARY: You're flirting!

HARRY: Oh, I wouldn't do it behind George's back.

MARY: No, you don't say much, Harry—but I did wonder—(*She touches her earrings*.)

85

HARRY: He's a lucky fellow. Yes, I was telling you—he took Prudence for a boat-ride on the Serpentine yesterday.

MARY: He what?

GEORGE: (*Free but strangled*) Yes, I was demonstrating the life-jacket and it all went very well, and suddenly I saw Prudence. Well, I took her for a paddle, just for a minute, and when she was getting out of the boat she slipped and fell in—I mean, got her shoes wet—so as it was cold, I suggested that she borrowed a pair of yours so she wouldn't get pneumonia, and we nipped back to the flat and she borrowed your shoes, I knew you wouldn't mind, of course—

HARRY: They all had a cup of tea.

MARY: All?

HARRY: She had some old people with her, according to George.

GEORGE: Yes—three or four, very nice old people—we all had a brew-up while Prudence was changing her shoes—cup of tea and a piece of cake—me and Prudence and some old folks, in the flat yesterday . . . I forgot to tell you.

HARRY: Old Pru certainly gets about. She's never at home. Just like George.

GEORGE: I meant to tell you—I say, Harry—you haven't got green on my teeth, have you?

HARRY: Only one of them—I told you not to move—

MARY: George—

HARRY: Don't you worry—it's lucky it's that one—

GEORGE: Why?—what's lucky about it?

(HARRY *inserts a clamp: this is a fitting like a tiny girder—the top and bottom hold apart the upper and lower jaw, preventing* GEORGE *from closing his mouth: which is wide open.*)

HARRY: I'm afraid he won't be needing it anyway.

MARY: Not that I care. Life-jackets.

HARRY: Fascinating job. Of course I'm very dull.

MARY: No, you're not, Harry.

HARRY: Nothing very romantic about dentistry.

MARY: But you're romantic at heart, Harry—that's what counts. You're a gentleman.

HARRY: I'm glad you liked the earrings.

MARY: Did you choose them, Harry?

HARRY: Yes—I really looked around for those. Actually, I didn't get around to mentioning it to Prudence—didn't want her to get any ideas—

MARY: What ideas would she get, Harry?

(HARRY *withdraws from* GEORGE's *mouth. They go out of his vision and their voices are off screen: we are left with* GEORGE's *eyes and gaping mouth.*)

HARRY: Oh . . . ideas . . .

MARY: You don't have ideas, do you Harry?

HARRY: Well, I'm only human. Aren't we all? George and Prudence and you and . . .

MARY: I'm only human—

HARRY: Of course you are, Mary . . . Are you sure those earrings aren't too tight—

MARY: Well, of course, being new . . .

HARRY: I was worried about that—there, does that pinch a bit—

MARY: It's slipped a bit, that's what it is—

HARRY: This way?

MARY: No, the other way, Harry . . . if you just push my hair back a little—

HARRY: Like this . . . ?

MARY: Can you see . . . ?

HARRY: Just turn your head a little—

MARY: Yes, Harry . . . that's better . . . that's nice . . .

(*The dialogue runs down to silence while we stay on* GEORGE's *face. His eyes move right and left. He tries to twist but he can't see behind the head-rest.*

Six or seven seconds of silence.

They come back into GEORGE's *view.* HARRY's *tie is almost under his ear.* MARY's *little white dental receptionist's cap is cock-eyed.* HARRY, *humming softly, fits the oxygen mask over* GEORGE's *face. Dissolve into* FLORA *and* AGNES *in the waiting room.*

There are two or three new people in the waiting room: old ill-kept faces. FLORA *and* AGNES *are sitting together as before.*)

FLORA: Oh, I could have had him—just like that—(*she snaps her fingers*)—he was begging me.

AGNES: I can see it now . . . On his knees.

FLORA: On his knees. I told him.

AGNES: You did.

FLORA: Straight out. I want a man who's all there.

AGNES: A whole man—

FLORA: I'm not interested in half a man, I said—

AGNES: You're right.

FLORA: Or three-quarters—a complete man is what I want. I want the lot and I can get it.

AGNES: I said to him—I don't care about how you *look* without them—(though he did look horrible)—that's not the point, it's the principle—

AGNES: That's it, I wouldn't have a man without them on principle—

FLORA: Because if *they*'ve gone already, what'll go next, I said.

AGNES: That's the point.

FLORA: (*Pause: sighs.*) Mind you, I was sorry. Six months later mine turned black. I would've had *any*body.

(*They sigh.*

The door to Mary's office opens. MARY *is there. Behind her* GEORGE *comes out of the surgery into the office, followed by* HARRY. GEORGE *is a stricken man.*)

MARY: Er . . . who was next?

(AGNES *and* FLORA *start telling each other to go first.*

We move through to GEORGE *and* HARRY.

GEORGE *moves.* MARY *turns to let him go by, but in the doorway*—)

(*Cool*) Did you say you'd be late again tonight?

HARRY: Same boat—It's dressmaking tonight . . . I wonder what she does with all the dresses she makes . . .

(GEORGE *is going.*)

Oh—by the way—I was going to catch up on the paperwork today—I was wondering if I could ask Mary to stay behind a while—as she knows the ropes . . . Would you mind, Mary—?

MARY: Oh no, that'll be all right—George is out tonight, he's tied up

HARRY: Well, take care, George—and don't forget—daily massage, get in there with the woodpoints.

(GEORGE *turns to face the patients who all stare at him with blank faces.* GEORGE *lets out a thin smile which is more like a wince. His middle tooth is missing. At this, all the patients smile at him, as one of their own. All around there are smiles like broken-down brooms.*)

Another Moon Called Earth

A Play for Television

Characters

PENELOPE
BONE
ALBERT
CROUCH
TV COMMENTATOR

1. INT. BONE'S STUDY. DAY
BONE *is working.*
PENELOPE: (*OV distant*) Dah-ling!
(BONE *takes no notice.*)
Dah-ling . . . .
(*He has heard but won't respond.*)
Help! Fire! Murder!
BONE: (*Murmurs*) Wolf . . .
PENELOPE: Wolves! Look out!! Rape! Rape! Rape!
BONE: Not the most logical of misfortunes.
PENELOPE: Go away, you brute! Don't force me! My husband will kill us both!
BONE: I do not insist on plausibility—
PENELOPE: Because I love him.
BONE: —Logic is all I ask.
PENELOPE: Oooooh . . . aaaah . . . I can't fight you any more— it's too lovely—oh—don't stop—ah—I don't care if he comes in—
(BONE *weakens, cracks and breaks. He slams down his pen, marches to her room.*)

2. INT. PENELOPE'S ROOM. DAY
TV set shows ceremonial parade.
PENELOPE: I think you owe me an apology.
BONE: Penelope, you know I can't have my work interrupted—
PENELOPE: Here you are, at the gallop—not bearing buckets of water—by no means with a poker raised to my defence—
BONE: Where's Pinkerton?
PENELOPE: —not a trace of aniseed dusted on your trousers to lure away the pack—oh no—

BONE: For God's sake—

PENELOPE: —as far as you're concerned, credibility begins with the thought of my unfaithfulness—

BONE: Penelope—

PENELOPE: How dare you?

BONE: I'm sorry—

PENELOPE: If that's what you think of me—

BONE: I don't—not for a moment did I think—

(*They have been competing with the television music.* BONE *turns it off. The music continues, fainter, but more real.*)

PENELOPE: Do you mind? There's going to be a commentary—

(BONE *goes to the window. The music drifts up.* BONE *stares down.*)

BONE: A parade . . .

PENELOPE: A parade . . . ! Where've you been for the last ten days?

BONE: Oh yes . . . the moon man. He's come back . . .

PENELOPE: The moon man? You make him sound like a piece of cheese. Don't you see he was the first? He's changed everything.

BONE: Well, he didn't discover it, after all. We all knew it was there. Nor did he have to navigate. He just—sat, really. And somebody had to be first. One thing leads to another; the last thing led to the moon. Logic. (*Peering out*) I can't see him . . . He must come near the end . . .

PENELOPE: You're such a fool—you should be down there cheering with all the rest. Can't you see he's smashed through?

(BONE *closes the window. He turns back from the window.*)

BONE: A cargo. He might have been a piece of cheese. He used to be a monkey. Before that he was a television camera. Now he is a man—but still a cargo. He sat. What else did he do?

PENELOPE: Isn't that enough? He stood off the world with his feet on solid ground, and brought everything into question—because up till then the world was all there was—and always had been—it was us and we were it—and every assumption was part of the world which was all there was, and is no longer—

(*He stares at her uncomprehending.*)

BONE: What did you want me for?

PENELOPE: I can't remember.

BONE: Well, I'll . . .

(PENELOPE *remembers.*)

PENELOPE: The window . . .

(BONE *goes to the window and opens it.*)

I wanted you to close the window . . .

(BONE *goes back and closes it.*)

BONE: Penelope, I've got to get on with my work.

PENELOPE: History! Do you think history matters now?

BONE: I do not write history, I dissect it—lay bare the logic which other men have taken to be an arbitrary sequence of accidents.

PENELOPE: Read me what you've done today.

BONE: You think in quantities. I am not a typist.

PENELOPE: You don't care that I'm ill.

BONE: Where's Pinkerton?

PENELOPE: I don't know.

BONE: It's her job to look after you.

PENELOPE: I let her go out to watch the parade.

BONE: She would have had a better view from the window.

(BONE *moves.*)

PENELOPE: Play with me—just till Albert comes.

BONE: Is he coming again?

PENELOPE: Why shouldn't he come?

BONE: Why should he?

PENELOPE: You resent me having visitors?

BONE: You don't have visitors. You have Albert. He never comes to see me.

PENELOPE: There's nothing the matter with you.

BONE: I don't like him.

PENELOPE: You don't know him.

BONE: So you entertain a man I don't even know?

PENELOPE: Entertain?

BONE: What am I supposed to think?

PENELOPE: What do you think?

BONE: I make no judgements. I'm asking you.

PENELOPE: Asking me what?

BONE: What would you think in my position?

PENELOPE: I don't think I like your tone. Albert is a very dear
friend, and it is natural that I should ask him to come and see
me. You have never bothered to emerge from your cave to
introduce yourself and now you ask why you don't know
him.

BONE: I can put two and two together, you know. Do not think
you are dealing with a man who has lost his grapes. Putting
two and two together is my speciality. I did not fail to notice
it when you began to receive visits from a handsome stranger
who arrived once or twice a week with an air of quiet
expectation, to leave an hour later looking more than a little
complacent—

PENELOPE: Albert's been coming to see me for months.

BONE: I did not leap to any hasty conclusion—I do not deal in
appearances, suspicions or wild surmise. I bide my time and
examine the evidence. But ten days ago you took to your bed
and remained there for no reason that has declared itself,
while at the same time, the stranger, Albert by name, began
calling every day. So I think it's time we had this out. There
is no doubt a logical explanation.

(*Starts to pace.*)

We have on the one hand, that is to say in bed, an attractive
married lady whose relations with her husband are, at their
highest, polite, and have been for some time. We have, on
the other hand, daily visits by a not unhandsome stranger
who rings the doorbell, is admitted by Pinkerton and shown
into the lady's bedroom, whence he emerges an hour or so
later and lets himself out. Now let's see, does anything
suggest itself? Wife in bed, daily visits by stranger. What
inference may one draw?

PENELOPE: Sounds to me that he's the doctor.

BONE: Doctor?

PENELOPE: What the hell did you think he was?

BONE: You mean you're ill?

PENELOPE: Good grief . . .

BONE: But he came before and you weren't ill then.

94

PENELOPE: How do you know? Perhaps I was being brave. You
  don't care! All you can do is accuse me—
BONE: Really, Penelope, I never—
PENELOPE: How could you—?
BONE: I made no accusations—I merely—
PENELOPE: You don't care that I'm not well—
BONE: How was I supposed to know you weren't well! I didn't
  know he was a *doctor*.
  (*She turns on the TV*.)
TV COMMENTATOR: . . . and what a magnificent occasion it is!
  Not even the rain can dampen the spirit here today as the
  people of London pay their homage to the lunanaut . . . and
  here comes the second rank of the Household Cavalry—I can
  see the glint of their brass as they come up out of Whitehall
  into the square followed by the massed bands of the Royal
  Air Force—Well, we still have some way to go before the
  high point of the procession, the golden capsule itself,
  reaches us here at—And here comes the fly-past of—!
  (*Jets roar in and whine away.*

  BONE *heads for the door*. PENELOPE *switches off the set*.)
PENELOPE: Darling . . . play with me . . .
BONE: I can't . . . I'm so behind . . .
PENELOPE: Oh, play with me.
  (*The jets reach the house, roar overhead and whine away.*)
BONE: You don't mean—? Do you mean?—Oh, Penelope . . .
  (*He reaches for her. She disengages herself peevishly.*)
PENELOPE: Oh, stop it! I meant play *games*.
BONE: Games.
PENELOPE: Amuse me. Jolly me along.
BONE: That's what Pinkerton's for.
PENELOPE: I got rid of her. Actually.
BONE: What do you mean?
PENELOPE: Gave her the push.
BONE: You didn't.
PENELOPE: This morning.
BONE: Why?
PENELOPE: Sudden impulse.
BONE: You can't.

95

PENELOPE: Did.

BONE: You must have had a reason.

PENELOPE: Felt like it.

BONE: A reason—

PENELOPE: Thirty-four years—suddenly it was quite enough.

BONE: She was your nanny—part of the family—

PENELOPE: Serve her right.

BONE: You can't just throw your old nanny into the street!

PENELOPE: Did. Well, she always won.

BONE: Won what?

PENELOPE: Everything! Every damn thing. Cards, noughts and crosses, charades—she had a mean winning streak, old Pinkers, so out she went.

BONE: I'm shocked.

PENELOPE: You'd think she'd have known something about the psychology of being a patient—but oh no! 'Oh, Penny, look at me, I've won again!'

BONE: What was behind it?—no such thing as pure impulse— yes, I'm shocked. And you need someone—I can't stop to— if you're going to stay in bed there's got to be someone—

PENELOPE: Albert will get me somebody. Albert would do anything for me.

BONE: Why, what do you do for him?

PENELOPE: Play with me.

BONE: What exactly is the matter with you?

PENELOPE: It hasn't got a name yet. I'm the first person to have it.

BONE: Measles? Yellow fever? Gastroenteritis?—what's the matter with you?

PENELOPE: Nothing, in here. I'm all right in bed.

BONE: I've got to work.

PENELOPE: Tell me about it!

BONE: Tell you . . . ?

PENELOPE: Entrance me! What are you on now?

BONE: I'm still on the Greeks.

PENELOPE: The Greeks! Warriors and poets! Lovers! Philosophers! Extending knowledge and empire—the rule of law and democracy!—sculptors in marble and gods in the image of man!

96

BONE: Yes, those Greeks.

PENELOPE: How far have you got?

BONE: The third century.

PENELOPE: You're catching up!

BONE: BC.

PENELOPE: Oh. But you've done the Etruscans.

BONE: Yes.

PENELOPE: The Etruscans! Mysterious shadows in the warm Italian stones that guard the secret of a vanished culture—a civilization under the olive hills!

BONE: (*Rises.*) Which explains nothing.

PENELOPE: Play! Here then—just one go. (*Pencils and paper.*) I'll be crosses, you be noughts.

BONE: Are you better today?

PENELOPE: I'm keeping my spirits up. Albert says that's the main thing.

BONE: Do you like him?

PENELOPE: He's all right in his way.

BONE: What way is that?

PENELOPE: Oh, you know.

BONE: No. What does he do?

PENELOPE: He's a doctor.

BONE: I mean—

PENELOPE: Three crosses! I won. You're better than Pinkerton.

BONE: I thought—

PENELOPE: At losing. Keep it up—remember what happened to her. (BONE *looks at her.*)

Only teasing, darling. Again!

BONE: Why does he bring you flowers?

PENELOPE: I'm a private patient.

BONE: You must be paying him a fortune.

PENELOPE: I've got a fortune.

BONE: Well, you never earned it, any more than me!

PENELOPE: Never said I did. But my daddy earned it more than your daddy earned it. Your go.

BONE: What does he do to you, Albert?

PENELOPE: He keeps my spirits up. My trouble is psychosomatic, you see.

BONE: Is it?

PENELOPE: Yes. I haven't actually got it, you see.

BONE: Got what!

PENELOPE: I've just got the symptoms.

BONE: Hysterical.

PENELOPE: Hilarious.

BONE: I meant—

PENELOPE: I've won again! Let's play battleships. Pinkerton sank my entire fleet in three minutes. That's really what did it, you know.

BONE: I think you should get up.

PENELOPE: I can't. I've lost the use of my legs.

(*She is preparing battleship papers.*)

BONE: That was very sudden.

PENELOPE: No it wasn't. It was very gradual. There, that's yours. Mark it one to eight down and A to H across. You're allowed four submarines, three destroyers, two cruisers and an aircraft-carrier. Put them anywhere you like.

BONE: I know how to play.

(*He marks his paper.*)

If you're not going to get any better we'll have to change your doctor.

PENELOPE: There's no question of my getting better. I can only hope to hold my own.

BONE: Does he ever mention me?

PENELOPE: Mmmmm, he says you're only half a man.

BONE: That's a filthy lie and you know it!—I am constantly repulsed—

PENELOPE . . . because every time he comes, he sees half of you, peering through the door. C-four.

BONE: What?

PENELOPE: C-four. Have I hit anything?

BONE: Oh. No.

PENELOPE: Your go.

BONE: B-six.

PENELOPE: No. G-two.

BONE: Submarine.

PENELOPE: Pow! Starboard torpedo away, sir! . . . Boom!

(*Distant gun booms.*)
We've got her! By George, we've got her! The sea is boiling
and here she comes up like a great wounded whale, and the
conning tower flies open and little men are jumping into the
sea!—Depth charges! Let go number one! Let go number
two!—Boom!
(*Distant gun again.*

BONE *rises.*

Third gun.)

BONE: What was that?

PENELOPE: The salute . . . Now they're saluting him . . .
(*Music in.*)

BONE: Are they going round the block?

PENELOPE: No!—the procession is miles long. They've got
eighteen different military bands and then there's the tanks
and everything, and the rocket-carrier with the capsule and
the lunanaut . . . . I want to see him—his face—I want to
see if it shows, what he has seen.

BONE: What?

PENELOPE: God, is it only me? I tell you, he has stood outside and
seen us whole, all in one go, little. And suddenly everything
we live by—our rules—our good, our evil—our ideas of
love, duty—all the things we've counted on as being absolute
truths—because we filled all existence—they're all suddenly
exposed as nothing more than local customs—nothing
more—Because he has seen the edges where we stop, and we
never stopped anywhere before—

BONE: Penelope—

PENELOPE: I'm telling you—when that thought drips through to
the bottom, people won't just carry on. The things they've
taken on trust, they've never had edges before.
(*Jets scream in over the house and whine away into the distance.*)

BONE: Oh come on now . . . Er, G-five.

PENELOPE: Nothing. H-three.

BONE: Nothing. A-four.

PENELOPE: Nothing. B-seven.

BONE: Nothing. E-six.

PENELOPE: Nothing. C-two.

BONE: Nothing. D-four.
> (*He has scored, it's on her face. Horror.*
> *The doorbell rings.*)

PENELOPE: Ding–ding–ding!
> Alarm stations, alarm stations! We've been hit—We're
> blowing up—Don't jump!—Don't jump—the sea's on fire.
> (*She throws herself back on the bed, hiding her face.*
> *The doorbell rings again.*
> *She lifts her face, smiling.*)
> That was close! Don't let him in till I'm ready.

3. INT. HALL. DAY

BONE *opens the front door.* ALBERT *is there, carrying an expensive
bunch of flowers.*

ALBERT: Good morning!

BONE: Good morning. Miss Pinkerton isn't here today.

ALBERT: I've come to see Mrs Bone.

BONE: Yes, I know. I was just saying Miss Pinkerton isn't here
today, that's all. I thought you may have been wondering
why she didn't open the door today.

ALBERT: Yes, I was wondering.

BONE: Well, she isn't here today.

ALBERT: Ah.

BONE: Well, this way! She won't keep you a moment.

4. INT. BONE'S STUDY. DAY

BONE: I'm Mrs Bone's husband.

ALBERT: Mr Bone.

BONE: Yes . . . Yes, I'm something of a logician myself.

ALBERT: Really? Sawing ladies in half—that kind of thing?

BONE: Logician. Well, sit down, sit down! My wife speaks very
highly of you.

ALBERT: And I'm very fond of her.

ALBERT:
BONE: How is she? (*Together*)

BONE: Well, you're the doctor—how am I supposed to know how
she is? She doesn't tell me anything. The first day she stayed
in bed I thought she'd had a bad night, and the next day I

thought—lazy old thing!—and—well, it's just gone on and on and there's no end to it. All she'll say is, she's all right in bed.

ALBERT: Yes, well, there's something in that.

BONE: You think so? I understand you're a good friend of hers.

ALBERT: Thank you. Is this where you do your work?

BONE: What?—Oh . . . yes. Yes, this is where I'm getting it all down. It's an immense undertaking, of course—

(ALBERT *is regarding the unkempt bed, turning over the blanket with his stick.*)

Yes—I bunk down in here—the midnight oil, you know— I've been bunking down in here since—well, it's my life's work of course.

ALBERT: Your life's work!

BONE: Yes. How long would you say I've got?

ALBERT: Are you inviting tenders?

BONE: No—just a professional estimate.

ALBERT: Well, I'd say as long as you've had.

BONE: (*Appalled*) Is that all? But I'm not half-way yet—not nearly.

ALBERT: What do you write?

BONE: It's sort of history.

ALBERT: What of?

BONE: The world.

ALBERT: The history of the world! How far have you got?

BONE: I'm doing the Greeks at the moment, third century.

ALBERT: Broken the back of them.

BONE: BC. But I've done the Etruscans.

ALBERT: Found plenty of new stuff, have you?

BONE: Well no, I mean practically nothing is known about the Etruscans. You see, I'm not exactly a *historian*—the actual history has all been written up by other people—but I'm discovering the patterns—exposing the fallacy of chance— there are no impulsive acts—nothing random—everything is logical and connects into the grand design.

ALBERT: Is there one?

BONE: There's got to be something going on besides a lot of accidents. If it's all random, then what's the point?

ALBERT: What's the point if it's all logical?

BONE: I hadn't meant to do a history of the world, only of myself . . . but the thing kept spreading, making connections back, wider and deeper all the time, the real causes, and suddenly I knew that everything I did was the culminating act of a sequence going back to Babylon . . .

PENELOPE: (*OV*) Dah-ling . . .

ALBERT: Ah! (*Moves.*) Mind you, this lunanaut—he'd make a good end to your book.

BONE: The lunanaut?

ALBERT: The logical place to stop, I would have thought. The day man bridged the cosmic gap. That was the day she took to her bed, you know.

(BONE *reacts.*)

PENELOPE: (*OV*) Dah-ling!

ALBERT: Well, if you'll excuse me—

BONE: (*Blocking his way*) What exactly do you do in there?

ALBERT: Well, I . . . examine her.

BONE: She won't let me examine her! You must have a good time, examining people.

ALBERT: Well, it's different for us medical men, you know. You think that when I'm examining Penelope—

BONE: Penelope?

ALBERT: Her name is Penelope, isn't it?

BONE: Yes.

ALBERT: She told me it was. You think that when I'm examining Penelope I see her eyes as cornflowers, her lips as rubies, her skin so soft and warm as milk . . . you think that when I run my hands over her back I am carried away by the delicate contours that flow like a sea shore from shoulder to heel— Oh, I know, dear fellow!—you think my mind turns to ripe pears as soon as I press those firm pink—

BONE: No, I don't!

ALBERT: But it's a misconception. To us medical men the human body is an imperfect machine constructed from cells, tissues, organs . . .

PENELOPE: (*OV*) Help! Fire, murder!

ALBERT: Funny thing, I knew a fellow called Bone once—I

wonder if he was a relation? Yes, he wanted to be an osteopath but he couldn't face the pleasantries—

5. INT. HALL. DAY

ALBERT: —which every patient would have felt obliged to make, so he took his wife's maiden name of Foot and now practises in Frinton as a chiropodist. My name is Pearce. Albert Pearce.

PENELOPE: (*OV*) Rape! Rape, rape!

ALBERT: I believe she's ready for me.

(*The doorbell rings.*

ALBERT *enters the bedroom, closing the door.*

BONE *answers the front door.* CROUCH *is standing there.*)

BONE: Yes?

CROUCH: Crouch, sir. Hall porter downstairs.

BONE: Is the lift out of order?

CROUCH: No sir, it's another matter I've come about.

BONE: You look as if you could do with a sit down.

CROUCH: You're right sir, thank you sir—It's a long haul.

BONE: Come this way. Did you want to see me?

CROUCH: Well, I'm seeing everybody, sir, making enquiries. You know what happened out there?

BONE: The parade?

6. INT. BONE'S STUDY. DAY

CROUCH: The incident. There's been a bit of an incident.

(*He sags into a chair.*)

Woman, middle-aged-to-elderly, five-foot-one, grey hair in a bun, blue dress, starched apron, fell in the street. Dead.

BONE: Oh . . . yes?

CROUCH: I've seen her coming in and out, but I've drawn a blank at the other flats. No one missing of that description here, sir?

BONE: Pinkerton . . .

CROUCH: Ah.

BONE: Oh dear . . . A small old-looking grey-haired lady in a white apron?

CROUCH: (*Takes off his peaked cap.*) Relative, sir?

BONE: My wife's nanny.

CROUCH: I've got to make a bit of a report, you see.

BONE: Yes . . . I'd better go and break the news . . . she'll be most upset.

CROUCH: Right, sir. I'll wait here.

(BONE *goes out.*)

7. INT. HALL. DAY

BONE *crosses hall, goes into bedroom.*

8. INT. PENELOPE'S ROOM. DAY

PENELOPE *is sitting up in bed.* ALBERT *is kneeling on the bed, kissing her chastely. He releases her and kneels back. They take no notice of* BONE.

PENELOPE: Do that last bit again.

(*He kisses her.*)

Pray-kiss?

ALBERT: No.

PENELOPE: Start again, from the beginning.

Tip-toe?

Slow?

ALBERT: (*A clue*) Ssssh!

PENELOPE: Quiet? Soft?

(ALBERT *nods.*)

Soft?

(ALBERT *grabs her.*)

Grab?

ALBERT: As if you were running away.

PENELOPE: Catch!

ALBERT: Y!

PENELOPE: Catchy?

(*He prays.*)

Priest? Pray? Monk?

(*He nods.*)

Monk!

(ALBERT *kisses her.*)

BONE: Softly softly catchee monkey.

ALBERT: Correct!

PENELOPE: Shut up! He spoilt it! What do you want?
BONE: Pinkerton's dead.
ALBERT: Dead!
BONE: There's a man come to make a report.
PENELOPE: What does he want to know?
BONE: I don't know.
PENELOPE: Well, it's a fat lot of good asking me, then, isn't it?
BONE: Monk-key. In the singular. Softly softly catchee monkey. Not monkiss.
ALBERT: Mr Bone, this is intolerable! I will not be interrupted in this frivolous manner while I'm bringing aid and comfort to a patient!

(BONE *retreats, closing the door.*)

9. INT. BONE'S STUDY. DAY

In the study CROUCH *is looking at one of Bone's notebooks.*

CROUCH: The Etruscans soon fizzled out, didn't they? I mean, there wasn't much *to* them. I never thought much of Eye-talians, mind you . . .
BONE: (*Briskly*) Mr Crouch, how exactly can we help you regarding this matter of Pinkerton's death? She was an old lady, rather frail. She fell down, fractured something perhaps—and died. It's very sad, but she had a splendid life in the best houses—what else can one say?
CROUCH: I thought you might know how it happened.
BONE: I thought she fell in the street?
CROUCH: From the window. We were all watching the parade and suddenly, behind us—thump . . . Amazing to think where he's been, the lunatic . . .

(*But* BONE *is already marching back to the bedroom.*)

10. INT. HALL. DAY

BONE *crosses hall to bedroom.*

11. INT. PENELOPE'S ROOM. DAY

BONE *storms in and stops dead.*
No one is in sight. The drapes are drawn round the bed. Albert's shoes, stick, hat and cape are lying neatly outside, on chair.

PENELOPE: (*Inside*) Who is it?

BONE: Me. How is she?

(PENELOPE's *head and bare shoulder appears.*)

PENELOPE: What?

BONE: I was asking how you were.

PENELOPE: What do you want?

BONE: He says Pinkerton fell from the window.

PENELOPE: Who does?

BONE: He says—

PENELOPE: I wish you'd shut up about Pinkerton! Go away!

(*She ducks back inside.*)

BONE: Well, it must have been your window—it's the only one overlooking . . . You can't hide!

PENELOPE: Hee hee hee, can't see me!

BONE: Who gave Pinkerton the push?

ALBERT: (*Within*) Say ninety-nine.

PENELOPE: Ninety-nine, doctor.

ALBERT: Feel any pain . . . there?

PENELOPE: No . . . no . . .

ALBERT: There?

PENELOPE: That's closer . . . down a bit . . . Yes, yes . . . Oh yes, that's it . . . yes, yes . . . yes . . . oh yes . . .

(BONE *retires.*)

12. INT. HALL. DAY

BONE *crosses*.

13. INT. BONE'S STUDY DAY

BONE: My wife's in bed with the doctor at the moment, Mr . . .

CROUCH: Crouch, sir. I see you're a historical man. I've got a historical turn of mind myself. Have you read *The Last of the Wine*?

BONE: Mr Crouch, let us not draw any hasty conclusions, let us be logical. Firstly, you say Miss Pinkerton fell from the window. Secondly, there is only one window overlooking the parade. Therefore—thirdly, my wife has lost the use of her legs, so—fourthly—Why didn't you take the lift as a matter of interest?

CROUCH: Ah, well, I was calling at every floor, you see, and it was always a case of just one more—but you're right, sir it does build up on you.

BONE: You could have taken the lift to the top and worked your way down.

CROUCH: By God, that's a brainwave you've got there.

BONE: Thank you. As you can see, I'm a cerebral man. I—fifthly, Miss Pinkerton was in service with my wife's family for thirty-four years and well loved—a second mother almost, certainly third or fourth—fifthly—sixthly—it's unthinkable.

CROUCH: Yes, it's a truly wonderful era, sir, for brains—they get you right to the top—take the loony—he's put us out of date—

BONE: Therefore—

CROUCH: Ah!

(ALBERT *has appeared, perfectly dressed once more.*)

ALBERT: Is this the fellow?

CROUCH: Good morning, sir.

ALBERT: Splendid. You examined the body?

(*He takes out a pad of certificates and starts scribbling.*)

CROUCH: I did have a look.

ALBERT: Well done. Eyes dilated?

CROUCH: Could well have been.

ALBERT: Excellent. Heart stoppage?

CROUCH: Not a flutter.

ALBERT: Adds up. Any signs of vertigo?

CROUCH: Well, she fell a long way.

ALBERT: Quite agree.

(*He tears off certificate, hands it to* CROUCH.)

Put yourself in my hands. No point in casting a shadow over a day of triumph.

CROUCH: Oh yes, sir—we better hurry if we want to see him.

14. INT. HALL. DAY

They move towards front door.

BONE: Just a minute—

ALBERT: Ah—yes, I think she's out of danger now. The main thing is—keep her amused. Humour her—plenty of fruit drinks—that kind of thing—

BONE: You think I'm a fool, don't you?

ALBERT: Mr Bone, medicine has many forms not given to the layman to understand—but we medical men have given up our youth to learn its mysteries and you must put your trust in us.

BONE: There's nothing wrong with her. When's she going to get up?

ALBERT: Get up? My dear fellow, Penelope can't get up. She's unable to leave her bed. I'm sorry, there's nothing I can do. She'll never walk again.
(*Briskly to* CROUCH) Come along, let's get this matter tidied up.
(*They leave.*

BONE *walks to bedroom door.*)

15. INT. PENELOPE'S ROOM. DAY
Sound of parade, cheering.

PENELOPE *is standing by the window, watching the parade. She does not look round.*

PENELOPE: There he goes . . . standing so straight and handsome in his yellow uniform . . . There goes God in his golden capsule. You'd think that he was sane, to look at him, but he doesn't smile because he has seen the whole thing for what it is—not the be-all and end-all any more, but just another moon called Earth—part of the works and no rights to say what really goes—he's made it all random.

BONE: She was your nanny.

PENELOPE: Poor Pinkers. You think I'm just a bad loser—but no one is safe now.

BONE: You can't hush it up, you know. And what about me? There's the law—accessory after the fact. You can't flout the laws—and nor can Albert.

PENELOPE: (*Fondly*) Huh—him and his ripe pears . . .

BONE: And don't think I don't know what's going on!

PENELOPE: Nobody knows except me, and him; so far. Albert almost knows. You'll never know. There he goes . . . .
(*She smiles. Waves her hand slightly at the lunanaut below.*)
Hello . . . .
(*The parade fades into the distance.*)

Neutral Ground

A Screenplay

Main Characters

PHILO—a native of Eastern Europe. Aged around 50, but looking older and more ravaged, especially in the later Montebiancan scenes

ACHERSON—a young, clean-cut Englishman, as they say. About 30, well educated

CAROL—about the same age. A competent, good-looking type

OTIS—American, ten years older, and ten years harder, conservative in appearance

LAUREL and HARDY—killers but fairly relaxed about it: they don't go around with grim poker-faces all the time

SANDERS—an up-and-coming Acherson

BOY—about ten years old, bright; simply dressed

And:

COMISKY—an American salesman

'LOCALS'—five travellers including a pretty girl

TRAIN POLICE

FRONTIER GUARDS

ASSASSIN

WAITER

NURSE

VET (WOLENSK)

MAID

MRS BUCHNER—a beautiful and rich lady

BORIS—the BOY's father

VILLAGERS

BOYFRIEND—for NURSE

BRIDE and GROOM

BOUNCERS—in discotheque

DESK CLERK—in hotel

MIDDLE-AGED WOMAN—in hotel

FOSTER — a diplomat

BARBER

PORTER

Montebianca is assumed to be a small country on the borders of Yugoslavia, consisting of a capital (also called Montebianca) and some outlying villages.

The village is very small, a few houses around a church and a bar.

1. EXT. OPEN COUNTRY. DAY. WINTER
An establishing shot of a passenger train.

2. INT. TRAIN. DAY
*The compartment is full, six passengers. Four of them are 'LOCALS',
including one pretty GIRL. The fifth is COMISKY, an American salesman.
The sixth is PHILO, who is distinguished from the others by his air of
slightly nervous reserve; by his clothes which suggest a bureaucratic
correctness despite being offset by a fur hat; and by his tiny pet monkey,
which peeps from his overcoat pocket.*
*It seems like a party, and COMISKY is the life and soul of it. The chatter
of the LOCALS is in a foreign tongue. A bottle is passed round. Fruit
and bread rolls are being shared. Only PHILO abstains. COMISKY
concentrates on the GIRL, who is wearing a fur hat much like
Philo's.*
COMISKY *takes her hat and puts it on his head. He prevents her from
snatching it back.*
COMISKY: I will take you home to America. I love you. Mrs
    Comisky will learn to love you, give her time.
    (*He brushes aside interruptions and defends the hat.*)
    I love you. Is this man your husband? Forget him.
    (*He kisses her hand gallantly. She snatches her hat back. He takes
    a swig from a proffered bottle.*)
    OK, at least let me take your hat to America. I want to buy the
    hat. I always wanted a fur hat.
    (*He takes out his wallet and from the wallet a note. The gesture is
    misunderstood. Ribald laughter and protest. The GIRL slaps him
    lightly.*
    PHILO *interrupts for the first time—tells the GIRL briefly, in her
    language, that the man just wants the hat. At this point* TWO

UNIFORMED OFFICIALS *enter and the* LOCALS *obviously know them well. Tickets and travel documents are offered. The cramped compartment is alive with chatter, the* OFFICIALS *joining in. The* GIRL *puts up with the flirting.*

PHILO's *document is obviously 'special'—it consists of several items, passport, letter, photo, identity card. The* OFFICIAL's *attitude changes into one of nervous respect which rapidly infects the other people, except* COMISKY *who remains oblivious until he is the only person left talking.* COMISKY *falls silent and looks round blankly.*)

Whassamatter . . . ?

(*The* OFFICIALS *salute* PHILO *and leave.* PHILO *strokes his monkey, and looks embarrassed.*)

3. EXT. FRONTIER STATION. DAY

A small frontier post, not even a village.
At one platform a train is waiting to leave, just beyond a guarded gate.
A few people in view, several in uniform.
In the distance our first train is approaching.

4. INT. TRAIN. CONTINUATION

Only COMISKY *and* PHILO *are left in the compartment.* PHILO *drinks from a small bottle of spirits, emptying it.*

COMISKY: You're coming all the way?

PHILO: Yes.

COMISKY: Sam Comisky—the New Jersey Comiskys, capitalists,— except the laundromat failed. You been in there on a trip?

PHILO: Yes.

COMISKY: It's a tight country for a salesman. I'm in and out.

(*The train brakes and slows.*)

The frontier. All change. I'll be glad to get back into Austria. How long was your visit?

PHILO: Fifteen years. Do you have by any chance some Austrian money—a coin for the public telephone?

(COMISKY *looks at him in surprise but fishes a fistful of coins out of his pocket.*)

COMISKY: Probably. There, how's that?

(*He gives* PHILO *a coin.*)

PHILO: Thank you. May I also make you a gift?
    (PHILO *takes off his fur hat and offers it to* COMISKY.)
COMISKY: Really? . . . Well, gee thanks.

5. EXT. FRONTIER STATION. DAY
PHILO, *with no luggage except a briefcase, hatless now, gets off the train
and walks rapidly towards the guarded gate, towards the waiting train.
Amid the other* PASSENGERS, COMISKY *follows carrying a suitcase and
the hat. He stops and puts the hat on.*
The Monkey climbs out of PHILO'S *pocket, up his coat.*
An ASSASSIN *is scanning the passengers, uncertainly, not sure of
himself.*
PHILO *is at the gate.*
The monkey with a little squeal jumps off PHILO *and scampers up*
COMISKY, *comically-angrily pulling at his hat.* COMISKY *laughs. The
monkey sits on* COMISKY'S *shoulder. The* ASSASSIN *sees* COMISKY *and the
monkey now.*
The ASSASSIN *produces a machine-pistol and starts shooting from close
range. It takes one long burst and then* COMISKY *and the monkey are
dead on the platform.*
PHILO *takes that in at a glance, and turns swiftly through the gate,
unnoticed. The* PASSENGERS *and* GUARDS *etc. scatter, some towards the
corpse.*
PHILO *pulls himself up into the waiting train.*

6. INT. STATION OFFICE. CONTINUATION
TWO GUARDS *stand nervously, holding guns, watching the* ASSASSIN.
The ASSASSIN *holds the phone to his ear and waits, drumming his
fingers on a piece of paper on the table. The paper is a snapshot, a
long-range blow-up of* PHILO *with the monkey on his shoulder. Behind
the* ASSASSIN, *the train with* PHILO *on it can be seen leaving the
station.*

7. INT. BIG RAILWAY STATION. DAY
Establish Vienna Station. Philo's train arriving.

8. INT. VIENNA STATION. CONTINUATION
PHILO *disembarks from the train.*

113

He is being covertly watched by two or three men. One of the men is
SANDERS; *another,* OTIS.

9. INT. PHONE BOX. VIENNA STATION. CONTINUATION
PHILO *studies the phone, etc., reading the instructions, holding*
Comisky's coin.
Cutaway: SANDERS *and* OTIS *watching.*
PHILO *dials.*
TELEPHONE: Toytown International.
PHILO: Toytown? Thank you. I want the Sales Director in charge
of train sets.
  (*A hand comes over* PHILO'*s shoulder and cuts off the call.* PHILO
  turns and sees SANDERS.)
SANDERS: I'm out.
  (OTIS'*s head joins him in the frame.*)
  This is Mr Otis of Model Aeroplanes. He's taken over
  Exports.

10. CREDITS

11. EXT. SMALL RAILWAY STATION. DAY
A third railway station. (The film is to end on a railway station, and
this plethora of stations is intended to top and tail the whole; thus it is
hoped that a virtue is made of the repetition.) This station is
Montebianca, clearly not much of a place.
A train has just arrived. Two men get off it: they will be referred to as
LAUREL *and* HARDY *whom they resemble in shape though not in*
amiability.
LAUREL *and* HARDY *each carry a small suitcase. They move slowly*
and deliberately, taking in the station as though it were a hotel room.

12. EXT. STATION BOOKSTALL. CONTINUATION
LAUREL *picks up a* Guide to Montebianca.

13. EXT. PAVEMENT CAFE. DAY
LAUREL *and* HARDY *sit at a table.* LAUREL *reads the guidebook.*
HARDY *sits with his fingers on a closed file lying in front of him on the*
table. They are in the same clothes as before—town suits, town shoes,

collars-and-ties, but slightly shabby. No suitcases now.

LAUREL: (*Reading*) 'The population of Montebianca is sixteen
thousand, five hundred.'

(*He looks around the café where a handful of people are sitting.*)

Sixteen thousand, four hundred and ninety-two to go.

(*The* WAITER *comes with their order of drinks which he places on
top of the file.* HARDY *carefully puts the drinks to one side.*)

HARDY: My friend, perhaps you can help me a little.

(HARDY *turns over the cover of the file, revealing a formal photo
of Philo, and a banknote.*)

I will be quite frank with you. It is a little matter of a
runaway husband. An old story. Maybe he is a customer
here?

(*The* WAITER *examines the photo.*)

It is not recent. He's missing for two years.

WAITER: Yes. Maybe I can help you a little.

(HARDY *gives him the banknote. The* WAITER *puts it in his jacket
pocket.*)

Yes, I can help you. Here he is definitely not a customer.

(*The* WAITER *smiles and goes about his business.* LAUREL *shakes
his head.*)

LAUREL: Sixteen thousand . . . Well, sooner or later they will all
walk past this table.

HARDY: Our orders are forty-eight hours.

LAUREL: Orders.

(*A* COUPLE *stroll past the table.*)

Sixteen thousand, four hundred and ninety.

HARDY: Does it say how many bars?

LAUREL: (*Looking through the guidebook*)

Probably a hundred.

(HARDY *downs his drink, closes the file and stands up.*)

HARDY: You see? The odds improve.

(LAUREL *also finishes his drink.* HARDY *moves out, having
dropped some money on the table.* LAUREL *makes a small detour
towards the* WAITER *who is balancing a laden tray on the tips of
his fingers.* LAUREL *approaches him smiling, dips his hand into
the* WAITER'*s pocket and retrieves the banknote. With his other
hand he delicately flicks the tray, sending it crashing to the floor.*)

LAUREL: Don't play games.
  (*He turns and follows* HARDY *away.*)

14. MONTAGE OF THREE BAR INTERIORS
LAUREL *and* HARDY *are having no success in their search for Philo.*
BARMEN *and* SERVING GIRLS *etc. are shown the photo but it means*
nothing to them.

15. INT. BAR
LAUREL: Why would he come here anyway?
HARDY: To drink.
LAUREL: No, to Montebianca. It's nothing, it's too small, it's not
    a country, it's a joke.
HARDY: Yes, it's a funny place.
LAUREL: It's a joke with postage stamps. Who wants it?
HARDY: Tourists. The mountains . . . very beautiful, they say.
LAUREL: Let's go. Maybe he's stopped drinking. Two years is a
    long time—many things about him must have changed.
HARDY: No, he drinks. I know them. Besides, what else do we
    know of him? Did you read the file? Half a sheet. How can
    we work from half a sheet on a whole man?
    (HARDY *looks around absently and notices at an adjoining table*
    an oldish man playing with a white kitten. HARDY *pauses on*
    that.)
    Zut!

16. INT. VETERINARY SURGERY. DAY
A cat in a cage. Then a line of cages containing puppies, birds, mice,
etc., with which LAUREL *is trying to ingratiate himself.*
LAUREL *and* HARDY *are alone in the room. The door opens and a*
NURSE *in white enters.*
NURSE: No, I'm sorry, Doctor Wolensk is operating just now.
HARDY: I just want the vet.
NURSE: Doctor Wolensk is the animal doctor.
HARDY: Oh. The *animal* doctor . . . Well, I'll just go and talk to
    him a minute.
    (HARDY *moves to the door.*)
NURSE: I'm sorry, it is not permitted—

116

(LAUREL *catches her by the arm, quite pleasantly.*)

LAUREL: He's an animal lover.

(HARDY *goes through the door. The* NURSE *tries to get free of*
LAUREL, *who pulls her up, not quite so pleasantly.*)

People he don't like so much.

17. INT. OPERATING ROOM. CONTINUATION

WOLENSK *is working over an unconscious dog. He looks up and sees*
HARDY.

WOLENSK: Who are you?

HARDY: I'm looking for a friend.

WOLENSK: There is no one here. Please leave.

HARDY: (*Sympathetically*) Oh! . . . A broken leg?

WOLENSK: That's right. A car accident.

HARDY: I would shoot him.

WOLENSK: (*Shocked*) Shoot the dog?

HARDY: No, the driver.

WOLENSK: (*Shouts*) Nurse! (*To* HARDY) Who gave you
     permission—?

(HARDY *takes out an automatic and examines it casually.*)

HARDY: No, I mean I'd really shoot him, I get so angry.

(WOLENSK *pauses and looks fearfully at* HARDY.)

This friend of mine has a monkey.

WOLENSK: What's his name?

HARDY: I don't know.

WOLENSK: You don't know your friend's name?

HARDY: Oh—I thought you meant the monkey.

WOLENSK: Look—what is this?

HARDY: Where do monkeys come from?

WOLENSK: Africa . . . South America . . .

HARDY: Yes. They are not native to Central Europe. There are no
     Austrian monkeys or Serbian, Bulgarian, no Montebiancan
     monkeys. Naturally. It gets too cold for them. And of course
     we do not have the jungle. Altogether, a monkey needs
     special attention here. Injections and so on. They would
     come to you; of course. You are the only vet. The only
     animal doctor, that is to say. My friend had another monkey
     but it died. A shooting accident. I think probably there is

another monkey now. Very very probably. If so, no doubt
you have done injections, and you can tell me where my
friend lives.

WOLENSK: Oh . . .

HARDY: By the way this gun is a toy, I do not really shoot
motorists.

(HARDY *puts the gun back in his pocket, rendering it harmless at
the psychological moment.*

WOLENSK *laughs his relief, laughs away his own foolishness for
being so frightened.*)

WOLENSK: Yes . . . Your friend lives in the Sondra Apartments,
top floor.

HARDY: Thank you, Doctor. By the way, what is my friend's
name?

WOLENSK: Buchner.

(*The illogicality of the question catches up on him, but* HARDY *has
gone.*)

18. EXT. SONDRA APARTMENT BLOCK. DAY
It is obviously fashionable and expensive. LAUREL *and* HARDY
approach it, and glance dubiously at each other, but go in.

19. INT. SONDRA APARTMENTS. DAY
The lift arrives at the top floor. LAUREL *and* HARDY *come out of the
lift. They are in a carpeted hall.*
HARDY *takes out his automatic and holds it down by his side.*
LAUREL *rings the doorbell of the penthouse.*
The door is opened by a uniformed MAID. LAUREL *and* HARDY *don't
like this.*

LAUREL: Mr Buchner at home?

MAID: Mrs Buchner?

LAUREL: Mr Buchner.

MAID: No Mr Buchner.

(HARDY *pushes past her and goes in.*)

20. INT. PENTHOUSE. CONTINUATION
As though he owns the place HARDY *throws open every door he sees.
Behind the third one is* MRS BUCHNER *in bed, sitting up and looking*

very beautiful in a negligee, eating breakfast off a tray and offering a spoonful of soft-boiled egg to her monkey.

21. EXT. SONDRA APARTMENT BLOCK. DAY
LAUREL *and* HARDY *walk out of the building.* HARDY *pauses on the pavement and furiously thumps his fist against the wall, and wonders what to do next.*
*Down the road comes a car, a smallish saloon, say a Fiat. It just goes past, but the occupants are featured—*ACHERSON *and* CAROL.

22. EXT. MONTEBIANCA. DAY
The Fiat drives out of the town.

23. EXT. COUNTRY ROAD. DAY
The Fiat in the distance, in bare, hilly country. Its approach is being watched by a BOY. *The* BOY *is with the camera on a hilltop. Down the opposite slope, in the valley, is the village. The car is heading towards the village.*

24. INT. CAR. CONTINUATION
CAROL *is looking at the guidebook.*
The road is a very bad one, narrow and rutted. The car bumps all the time and has to go quite slowly.
CAROL: Nice to get off the beaten track.
     (ACHERSON *is silent.*)
     It says the views are unexampled by the largest traveller.
ACHERSON: Views of what?
CAROL: I don't know. Do you want to stop for a while?
ACHERSON: Why?
CAROL: *Why?* We're supposed to be on holiday. What's the
     matter?
ACHERSON: Nothing's the matter. I'm not in a holiday mood.
     Besides, I'm combining it with business, aren't I? I'm taking
     the little woman on a sales trip. Nice hotel, exotic food,
     unexampled views, all on the firm. A perk.
CAROL: Who'd send a salesman to Montebianca?
ACHERSON: We would. It's off the beaten track. Tell me, do you
     fancy Giles Foster?

119

CAROL: Yes, I do rather.

ACHERSON: I thought you did.

CAROL: I thought you thought I did. (*Pause.*) Were you really at school with him?

ACHERSON: Yes.

CAROL: Well, he's doing quite well. I hope you're not going to spoil my holiday.

25. EXT. THE ROAD. CONTINUATION

The BOY, *in the same position, watches the car, which is too far away to be audible. Then he turns and starts making his way quickly down the opposite slope, descending towards the village.*

26. EXT. THE VILLAGE. CONTINUATION

The BOY *runs into the village. He goes into the bar.*

27. INT. BAR. CONTINUATION

The bar is almost empty. The boy's father (BORIS) *is the barman. He is talking to the only* CUSTOMER. *The* BOY *goes past them, through a door and then up the back stairs.*

28. INT. PHILO'S ROOM. CONTINUATION

PHILO *is asleep on an unkempt bed in an unkempt room. He obviously has few possessions; but one of them is a monkey. The* BOY's *knock is heard. The monkey wakes* PHILO. *The* BOY *opens the door and comes in.*

BOY: Captain! Somebody comes.

PHILO: (*Waking*) Hah?

BOY: A car comes. You said to wake you any time—

PHILO: Yes. Who comes?

BOY: A car. A Fiat, I think.

PHILO: So?

BOY: You told me—

PHILO: Yes. How many people?

BOY: I don't know. I was on the hill. I ran here.

PHILO: Of course. My good scout.

BOY: Maybe only a tourist. They get lost.

PHILO: Of course. They will drive through to Zlens. Tell me if

they stop, eh? If it's children in the car it's all right. Tell me
if it's just men. Anything funny, you tell me, eh?

BOY: Yes, Captain. Who do we wait for?

PHILO: I tell you, it could be a bishop and his grandmother, or the
last man in the Tour de Monte bicycle race. But probably
there is no need for play-acting. Probably he will look like a
debt collector. A debt collector can be any man in a suit and a
car. Tell me if it stops.

BOY: He wishes you to pay a debt?

PHILO: Yes.

BOY: But you do not wish to pay it?

PHILO: If it can be avoided. I do not owe it. Do you see?

BOY: Of course. Will you buy me a gun?

PHILO: What do you want a gun for? This is not cowboys. (*He
picks up the monkey.*) Oh no, it is not cowboys.

29. INT.   HOTEL ROOM.   IN THE TOWN.   DAY
Laurel's and Hardy's room.
LAUREL *lies on his back on one of the twin beds.* HARDY *paces up and
down.*

LAUREL: Books. The library.

HARDY: For me it's still the monkey. For ten years in Moscow he
keeps a monkey. Maybe the monkey is the only friend he
trusted, a man in his position. Now he is alone somewhere. I
see him with a monkey. We'll try the pets' doctor again.
Show him the photo.

LAUREL: *Now* you show him the photo . . . (*He laughs shortly.*)

HARDY: Who would expect two people with monkeys in a place
like this?

LAUREL: Not me. A monkey is a risk for him. 'Look at that man,
he has a monkey,' . . . no.

HARDY: After a while a man takes risks. Two years now. He
thinks he is well hidden. Maybe even forgotten. He needs a
friend who asks no questions. I think we visit the animal
doctor.

LAUREL: No, the animal nurse. You spoiled the doctor. Next time
if he has any more friends with monkeys he will say nothing
and then telephone.

30. EXT. VILLAGE. DAY

ACHERSON *and* CAROL *walk into the village. They are objects of great curiosity. It is not the kind of village which is used to tourists.*
VILLAGERS, *mainly children and old people, emerge and watch them.*

31. INT. PHILO'S ROOM. CONTINUATION

PHILO *sees this from the window.* ACHERSON *starts talking to one of the* VILLAGERS.
The BOY *enters the room urgently.*

PHILO: Yes—I see them. I don't like this walking.
    (*Cutaway to* ACHERSON.)

ACHERSON: It's very simple. I want—to buy—money—look, I
    have money—I want to buy *petrol.* Auto er no go, halt.
    (*Nobody understands him.* BORIS *shows up and gestures*
    ACHERSON *and* CAROL *to enter the bar.*
    Finish cutaway.)

BOY: Tourists. English.

PHILO: Yes. I suppose so.

BOY: My father is bringing them. What shall I do, Captain?

PHILO: Nothing. Yes—take Mimi. In your room.
    (*He gives the* BOY *the monkey, and the* BOY *goes out.* PHILO *takes*
    a big drink, pouring from a bottle into a dirty glass. There is a
    knock on the door, and BORIS *shows in* ACHERSON *and* CAROL,
    with a flourish.)

BORIS: Anglitch!

ACHERSON: I say, do you speak English?

PHILO: Yes.

ACHERSON: Thank the Lord for that. We've run out of petrol,
    about a mile down the road, if you can call it a road.

PHILO: You were coming here?

ACHERSON: No. Well, we weren't going anywhere in particular.
    Just having an afternoon off . . . a bit of a tour . . . the
    views, and all that.

PHILO: An afternoon off?

ACHERSON: We're in Montebianca, for the week; business and
    pleasure, sales and marketing—last year was Majorca,
    frightful place, but it gets you away—

CAROL: Charles . . .

ACHERSON: Oh yes—getting off the point. My name's
Acherson . . . My wife, Carol.

CAROL: How do you do?—We'd be awfully grateful if you . . .

PHILO: You ran out of petrol just from Montebianca?

ACHERSON: We hired the car there, paid for it to be topped up—
they're all such thieves. They took me for just another stupid
tourist. Well, they won't get away with it. I've got
connections at the Consulate. Look—is there any petrol in
the village?

PHILO: No, no cars, no tractors. The fields are too rocky, they use
horses.
(*He speaks briefly to* BORIS *who replies.*)
Yes, there's a pump four miles back where you turned off the
main road. He'll send someone to get a can for you.

ACHERSON: Thank you. Can you tell him we'll pay for the trouble.

PHILO: He knows that.
(BORIS *leaves the room.*)

ACHERSON: Well, we mustn't impose on you.

CAROL: No. Is there a bathroom?—I could do with a bit of a . . .

PHILO: (*Suddenly deciding to accept them*) There's clean water in
the jug. Please avail yourself. The towel's clean, too—you're
lucky; I count the weeks by clean towels.

ACHERSON: Have you been here long?

PHILO: Yes.

ACHERSON: Well, the simple life. I must say I quite envy you.

CAROL: (*Pouring water*) At the hotel he made a fuss because the
claret wasn't château-bottled.

ACHERSON: Well, one must draw the line . . . . You're not
English, are you?

PHILO: No.

ACHERSON: It's our first time here. Always been curious to see the
place. Beautiful country, charming people—

CAROL: He can't stand it—

ACHERSON: Now hold on, Carol . . .

PHILO: I can't stand it either.

ACHERSON: Frightful hole, isn't it? Why don't you leave?

PHILO: I have a problem with papers.

ACHERSON: Oh yes . . . they're very keen on papers. Well—

(*He turns to* CAROL *who is drying her hands.*)

PHILO: Did you find soap?

CAROL: Yes, thank you. Where should I empty the water?

PHILO: It's all right.

CAROL: Well, thank you.

ACHERSON: We'll be in the bar. Might see you there. Perhaps we could buy you a drink before the fellow comes back with the petrol.

PHILO: Yes. Thank you. I usually have a glass or two around this time.

ACHERSON: Fine.

(PHILO *closes the door after them, and sits down on the bed. He laughs to himself, at himself, and has a drink on himself.*)

32. EXT. MONTEBIANCA TOWN. SHOPS CLOSING. LATE AFTERNOON

LAUREL *and* HARDY *are watching the vet's door. One or two cars are parked around there.* LAUREL, *bored, is glancing at the guidebook. He starts to laugh.*

LAUREL: Hey, it mentions you. The views are unexampled by the largest traveller.

(HARDY *glowers at him.*

Up the road, the NURSE *comes out of the vet's. She walks away from them, and they start to move. But after three paces she stops and gets into the front passenger seat of a waiting car.* LAUREL *and* HARDY *look round helplessly but this is not a taxi-laden place.*

The NURSE *is seen to kiss the* BOYFRIEND *as the car moves.* HARDY *throws his hat on the ground.*)

33. INT. VILLAGE BAR. LATE AFTERNOON

BORIS *behind the bar. Some* LOCALS. PHILO, ACHERSON *and* CAROL *share a table and a bottle. The* BOY *enters, carrying a two-gallon can with some difficulty. He stops when he sees the three of them together.*

PHILO: Here!—S'okay.

(*It is apparent that* PHILO *is looser through drink. The* BOY *sees now that* CAROL *is holding Mimi the monkey.*)

They are friends. (To CAROL) Here is my other friend—in fact he is my scout.

CAROL: He's a scout?
>(*The* BOY *smiles but is disappointed by* PHILO. ACHERSON *gives the* BOY *money which the* BOY *gives to* BORIS. PHILO *explains this—*)

PHILO: His father.

ACHERSON: Oh. Well, are you ready, Carol?

CAROL: I'll wait for you here, darling. You'll be back in half an hour.

ACHERSON: Well, come for the walk.

CAROL: No, I've walked enough. You've got to drive past this way so you might as well pick me up.
>(*He's not sure about it.*)

Honestly, I'll be perfectly all right.

ACHERSON: Fine. Well, see you both later.

CAROL: Bye bye, darling.
>(CAROL *gives Mimi to* PHILO *and gets up to see* ACHERSON *to the door.* ACHERSON *goes. Mimi sits on* PHILO's *shoulder.* PHILO *pours a drink.*
>*There is a flash.* CAROL *has taken his picture. The camera was in her shoulder bag.*)

PHILO: (*Sharply*) What are you doing?

CAROL: What's the matter?
>(*Everybody in the bar looks at* CAROL.)

I like to take pictures. Is it all right?

PHILO: (*Subsiding*) Yes . . . of course.

CAROL: I'd like to take some in the village.

PHILO: Yes. Why not?

34. EXT. VILLAGE. THE CHURCH. LATE AFTERNOON
A wedding is taking place.
A BRIDE *and* GROOM *and* WEDDING GUESTS *come out of the church with much gaiety.*
CAROL *takes a picture.*
CAROL *moves around the village looking for and finding picturesque subjects. She is watched by not particularly friendly faces of* WOMEN.
CAROL *sees* PHILO *watching her from his upstairs window. She waves at him cheerfully. She raises the camera to her eye, but through the lens she sees his window empty.*
The shadows lengthen.

35. EXT. ROAD. CONTINUATION

ACHERSON *walks along the road. There is no one in sight. Then* ACHERSON *gets the feeling he is being watched. He looks around. Perhaps he hears a sound. The surroundings begin to look sinister to him. He hurries on towards the car. Then he definitely sees something move, off the road, behind rocks. He puts the can down quietly and moves off the road and waits. After a moment he moves aside quietly and then changes direction back towards the road. Ahead of him, his back to* ACHERSON, *the* BOY *reveals himself.*

ACHERSON: (*Relieved*) Hey!—You scouting?

(*The* BOY *looks at him, embarrassed.*)

Come on then.

(*The car is only yards away.* ACHERSON *gets the can. The boy takes the cap off the tank, and* ACHERSON *pours the petrol. When the can is empty,* ACHERSON *puts it into the car. The* BOY *screws the cap on the tank.*

There is the sound of petrol trickling. ACHERSON *sees petrol on the road and realizes the tank is holed.*

The BOY *is paying no attention. On the back window-ledge of the car, among boxes and odds and ends, he sees part of a rifle.*)

36. INT. VILLAGE BAR. LATE AFTERNOON

PHILO, *without Mimi, is drinking.* CAROL *comes in and puts the camera on the table in front of him.*

CAROL: Hello.

PHILO: Mrs . . . I've forgotten your name.

CAROL: Acherson.

PHILO: Mrs Acherson . . . It's very nice for me that you ran out of petrol. I don't see many people . . .

CAROL: You didn't seem very pleased at first.

PHILO: I didn't know who you were . . . You could have been . . . anybody.

CAROL: Well, we were.

(*She smiles at him.*)

PHILO: What does your husband do?

CAROL: He's a sales executive.

PHILO: What does that mean? A salesman?

CAROL: I suppose so. He never discusses work at home. I suppose he's just a salesman.

PHILO: He said he had connections. At the Consulate.

CAROL: Oh that. A school friend. Charles was just bad-tempered about the car. He isn't frightfully good about Abroad. Last year the Spaniards were dirty, the year before the French were grasping and the year before that the Italians were impertinent. Now the Montebiancans are all thieves—oh, I say, you're not—?

PHILO: No, I'm not.

CAROL: Well, what are you?

PHILO: We're not on the maps any more. The Russians, you know . . . They saved us in the war, that's how it started, and now they have saved us out of existence. I'd like to go back while my own language is still being spoken. But I can't leave here.

CAROL: Did you choose to come?

PHILO: Choose? I don't know. It's neutral ground. They let me in and they let me stay.

CAROL: What do you do?

PHILO: Drink. I have some savings, in the bank in town. I write Boris a cheque once a month.

CAROL: And when the money's gone?

PHILO: When the money's gone I'll be dead, if I time it right. What does your husband sell?

CAROL: Toys.

(*This naturally brings* PHILO *up short.*)

PHILO: Toys?

CAROL: Yes, that's right. Toytown International. He's on the export side.

(PHILO *stares at her.*)

37. MIX TO REPRISE, SCENE 9

TELEPHONE: Toytown International.

PHILO: Toytown? Thank you. I want the Sales Director in charge of train sets.

(SANDERS *cuts off the call.*)

SANDERS: I'm out.

(OTIS *joins him in the frame.*)

This is Mr Otis of Model Aeroplanes. He's taken over Exports.

OTIS: Welcome to Vienna, Mr Marin.

SANDERS: Mr Otis is an American. I'm afraid.

OTIS: I'm attached to London. Just happened to be visiting. Kind of lucky.

38. EXT. VIENNA STATION. CONTINUATION

PHILO, SANDERS *and* OTIS *walk out of the station and into a waiting car, all three men getting into the back.*

39. INT. CAR. CONTINUATION

The car moves off through the city.

SANDERS: My name is Sanders. A friend of a friend called from the frontier. Pity about the trouble. Who was it?

PHILO: An American salesman. Comisky, I think. Poor man. They killed my monkey, too.

OTIS: Your monkey, Mr Marin?

PHILO: I couldn't leave Nana behind—I'd had her for years.

OTIS: That's an exotic sort of pet, Mr Marin. You must have felt pretty secure.

PHILO: Why not?

OTIS: But at the frontier . . .

PHILO: I don't understand it.

SANDERS: They must have known you were doing a bunk. They were waiting for you.

PHILO: I don't know—I've been thinking, perhaps it *was* Comisky they wanted—perhaps he was—somebody in the game—a bizarre coincidence . . .

OTIS: (*Coldly*) They were waiting for you. Think about it, Marin. Just stay quiet and think about it.

PHILO: (*To* SANDERS) Who is this man? I want to see Brigadier Payne in London. I work for *him*. And him I trust.

SANDERS: He's Major-General Payne, Retired. Retired to his club where he reads *The Times* through a magnifying glass, I'm told. The old soldiers have gone, and the professionals are in charge.

OTIS: You've been away a long time, Marin, and for the last four years you've been working for me. And at the moment I don't even know if you are who you are supposed to be,

128

because you're supposed to be dead, you and your monkey. (*The car stops outside an old nondescript building.*)

40. EXT. CAR. CONTINUATION
The three of them get out of the car and enter the building. Outside the main door there is a brass plate: Toytown International.

41. INT. TOYTOWN OFFICE. DAY
A simple room. Sanders's office.
SANDERS *sits behind the desk.* PHILO *stands.* OTIS *is not there.*
PHILO: You take your orders from an American?
SANDERS: I wouldn't put it like that. It's liaison, common interest. There's been a merger. None of us likes it. Otis reports to a committee of three, one of whom is a German. Funny old world. I can tell you that because the German's mistress ran off to Moscow with the Naval Attaché. But I suppose you'd heard.
PHILO: No, I hadn't. Brigadier Payne was kicked out?
SANDERS: Decent sort, Payne. Trouble was he bumped off a couple of Washington's lads in East Berlin—the Americans' own fault, in my view, since they never told us what they were about, but the result was this idiotic combined ops, and I have to take orders from Otis. Though I wouldn't put it like that. He's top man for the toy factory now as far as Clearance goes. I'm told he's a decent sort when you get to know him, but no one ever has, so his decency is a sort of secret.
PHILO: Have you got a drink in here?
SANDERS: Heavens, no.
PHILO: Well, what happens now?
SANDERS: What did you want?
PHILO: I want to go back to England.
SANDERS: To the office?
PHILO: I don't know.
SANDERS: Nor me. It's not like it was with Payne.
PHILO: I had a right to leave, Sanders.
SANDERS: You were working for us.
PHILO: I'm not a British agent. I don't belong to anybody.
(OTIS *enters, carrying a file.*)

I don't owe you people a thing.

OTIS: An explanation, Philo.

PHILO: Oh—so I'm not dead?

OTIS: Your prints came through for you.

(*He tosses a fingerprint card on the desk.*)

Well, now. What brings you to Vienna?

PHILO: (*Shrugs.*) You had a friend inside. One day he had enough.

OTIS: Why?

PHILO: That would take a lot of explaining.

OTIS: Well, I'd like to take your explanation back to London, and I'm leaving tonight.

PHILO: Without me?

OTIS: That depends. Why did you have enough?

PHILO: Look, I wasn't in it for your country. I had my own.

OTIS: Common interest.

PHILO: That may have been so in the old days. Now my country doesn't even show on *your* maps. The tanks have been followed by the map-makers, and in the schools the children are only taught Russian. I wasn't doing any good in there. I was doing more before.

OTIS: (*Angrily*) What—with that sad little group of émigrés keeping the flag flying from a maisonette in Notting Hill? That's where Payne took you from, Marin, and it's a lot sadder now with their photographs of dead generals and their middle-aged amateurs getting picked up in Leningrad with their coat linings stuffed with leaflets. Leaflets! Don't tell me you came back for that?

PHILO: No.

OTIS: What then?

PHILO: Listen, Otis. They've got away with it. My war is lost. It was probably lost before I joined it. And I'm tired of fighting in yours.

OTIS: That's why you got out?

PHILO: Yes.

OTIS: Just like that? Catch a train in Moscow, change here and there, across borders, everything smooth, no questions, all the way to the frontier. And then they shoot the wrong man.

PHILO: That's right.

OTIS: Most people have more trouble.

PHILO: Most people would. Listen, Otis, back in the East you can't do much without the right papers, but *with* the right papers you can do *anything*. They *believe* in papers. Papers are power. And my job was papers.

OTIS: And the shooting?

PHILO: I don't know—I'll never know.

OTIS: What do you want, Marin?

PHILO: I want a home. A country. I think you owe me that.

OTIS: I don't owe you a thing except your gratuity, and that's in the bank.

PHILO: I don't want it. I want nationality, Otis.
(OTIS *regards him coolly.*)

OTIS: We've got papers too, you know.

42. EXT. DISCOTHEQUE. NIGHT
LAUREL *and* HARDY *have found the car. Parked. Empty.*

43. INT. DISCOTHEQUE. CONTINUATION
LAUREL *and* HARDY *find the* NURSE *dancing with her boyfriend, two rockers in a room jammed with rockers.* LAUREL, *with old-world courtesy, 'cuts in', a custom clearly new to the* BOYFRIEND *who would resist but* HARDY *gathers him in a friendly embrace with a hearty cry of recognition. The* BOYFRIEND *protests.* HARDY *kisses him on each cheek, and lifts him an inch off the floor and moves him like a shop-window dummy behind a pillar and puts him down. The* BOYFRIEND *hits* HARDY *who starts a casual sort of fight which quickly achieves* HARDY's *intention: two* BOUNCERS *converge on* HARDY *and the* BOYFRIEND *and expel them from the premises.* HARDY *plays it soft.*

44. EXT. DISCOTHEQUE. CONTINUATION
HARDY *and the* BOYFRIEND *are shoved out by the* BOUNCERS. HARDY *shakes himself loose, and lights a cigar, offering one to the* BOYFRIEND. *The* BOYFRIEND *swings at* HARDY *who massacres him in a few seconds.* HARDY *settles against the wall to wait for* LAUREL.

45. INT. DISCOTHEQUE. CONTINUATION
Everybody is dancing appropriately to the rock music, except LAUREL

who is firmly foxtrotting with the helpless and bewildered NURSE.

NURSE: What do you *want*?

LAUREL: I have a message from a friend. He asked me to give you this.

(*In his 'leading hand', the one holding her hand, he is clutching the photo of Philo; he turns the photo towards her.*)

NURSE: What's that?

LAUREL: You know him. Think back.

(*The gamble pays off.*)

NURSE: Oh yes. What do I want with a picture of Mr Kramer?

LAUREL: Kramer. Exactly. He brought his monkey to the animal doctor and instantly he was in love.

NURSE: Monkey? What monkey? I knew him when I worked in the library. That was a year ago.

LAUREL: The library, by all the saints. (*Pause.*) He lived near the library?

NURSE: In the Olympia Hotel. I was always sending him reminders.

LAUREL: Reminders?

NURSE: For the books. Where is my friend? Will you stop making this stupid dance, you make me ridiculous.

LAUREL: Listen, you're dancing with a genius. (*He shakes his head scornfully.*) Monkey . . .

46. INT. FOYER OF OLYMPIA HOTEL. NIGHT

LAUREL *and* HARDY *arrive. It's a small hotel, and there is only a* DESK CLERK *around.* LAUREL *is still smirking and laughing to himself.* HARDY *looks grim. They arrive at the desk.*

CLERK: Good evening.

HARDY: What room is Mr Kramer?

CLERK: Kramer? There is no Mr Kramer.

(HARDY *reaches out for the* CLERK's *throat, drags him over the counter, and stands him up.*)

HARDY: Do not tell me there is no Mr Kramer.

LAUREL: (*Amused*) The one with the monkey.

CLERK: Oh—*him.*

(*The smile drops off* LAUREL's *face.* HARDY *turns to look at him expressionlessly.*)

HARDY: Yes. Him.

47. INT. THE BAR. EVENING
Some kind of bar game going on. Skittles perhaps. CAROL *is watching it.* LOCALS *playing and drinking. She reaches for her camera to take a picture, starts to check that she's turned the film on; pauses, frowns at the camera. She opens the camera: there is no film in it now.*

48. EXT. COUNTRYSIDE. EVENING
PHILO *is moving rapidly towards the car, short-cutting across rocks. From behind a rock, a rifle pokes at him.*
Close-up of trigger being squeezed.
It's a cap-rifle. The BOY *stands up gleefully. He's got a cowboy hat on, too.* PHILO *turns the other way and sees* ACHERSON.

ACHERSON: Hello, old man. Bad news.

PHILO: The car will not take you away after all.

ACHERSON: Right. Tank's holed.

PHILO: Of course. You're bad news for me, Acherson.

ACHERSON: How's that, old man?

> (PHILO *goes up to the car and looks in. He takes out one of the boxes lying on the back seat. The box has a picture of a train set and some writing.* PHILO *looks at the box and tosses it back.*)

PHILO: So you're in the toy business.

ACHERSON: That's it. Santa Claus.

PHILO: You might as well go home.

ACHERSON: Old man, I don't understand you at all. How far is that garage?

PHILO: (*Pause.*) It's not a garage. It's a pump.

ACHERSON: This is a welding job. It seems we're here for the night.

> (ACHERSON *moves to walk back.*)

PHILO: Acherson!—you're wasting your time! I don't owe you people a thing!

ACHERSON: Anything you say, old man.

> (ACHERSON *strides off.*)

BOY: Is he the debt collector?

PHILO: No—not the one I feared. This one I despise.

49. INT. CONTINUATION OF FLASHBACK
Two locomotives race past each other.
It's a toy train set, or rather several of them combined into an extensive

layout, on the floor of a store room which contains many boxes of toys including boxes identical to the one seen in Acherson's car in the last scene.

PHILO *is playing trains.*

The door is audibly unlocked and opened.

PHILO: (*Without turning round*) I'm not hungry, take it away.

(*But it's* OTIS, *accompanied by* SANDERS.)

OTIS: Well, you've managed to pass the time, I see. I'm glad *somebody* plays with the window-dressing.

PHILO: Where've you been?

OTIS: Taking a personal interest, in London.

(OTIS *gets interested in the train set and squats down to mess with it. Pretty soon trains are whizzing round with* OTIS *working the points as he talks.*)

PHILO: I could have come with you.

OTIS: On your papers?

PHILO: Next time I'll come out with a British passport and a working permit. Look, can't we just go and discuss it over a drink somewhere?

OTIS: As of now you're free. Sorry it took so long.

PHILO: Free? Free to do what? Go where?

OTIS: Home.

PHILO: London?

(OTIS *looks at him.*)

OTIS: Home.

PHILO: What are you talking about? You know what would happen to me if I went back there . . . God, I need a drink . . .

OTIS: What made you hit the bottle?

PHILO: Hit the bottle?

OTIS: You made a fool of yourself at a public dinner on the seventh; you were drunk at a reception for the Polish delegation the week you came out, and at another for the Bulgarians the week before that. It seems you even drank in your office. Why was that?

PHILO: Well, I congratulate you. I also drank in bed. Did no one tell you?

OTIS: Why?

(SANDERS *has squatted down and is messing with the trains but he gets the points switched wrong and there is a minor derailment.*)
(*Irritably*) Sanders, what the hell do you think you're doing? (*To* PHILO) Why?

PHILO: Nerves.

OTIS: What did you have to be nervous about?

PHILO: That's a damn silly question.

OTIS: *What were you nervous about?* (*Pause.*) You were all right. A comrade. Good record. Impeccable behaviour. Regular promotion. Suddenly you had nerves.

PHILO: I had decided to get out.

OTIS: Why?

PHILO: I told you.

OTIS: Speeches. Speeches about maps and schoolchildren. Why did you get out?

PHILO: Otis, I'm not talking to you any more.

OTIS: And *how* did you get out?
(*For this he abandons the train set and looks straight into* PHILO's *eyes.*)
Think before you reply. The right answer might get you where you want to go.

PHILO: I'm telling you the truth. I told you why and I told you how.

OTIS: You gave yourself false papers.

PHILO: Not false. The real thing, falsely obtained. That's a trick which perhaps only one man in the country could have played, and only once, but I was the man.

OTIS: It sounds plausible. It might even have been possible.
(*He spells it out now.*)
Only you were already blown.

PHILO: (*Total disbelief*) No.

OTIS: You were blown.

PHILO: I tell you I wasn't.

OTIS: How long had they been on to you?

PHILO: If they were on to me I didn't know it.

OTIS: You knew it because they told you.

PHILO: *No!* They had nothing on me! For God's sake I was sending you stuff almost to the week I left.

135

OTIS: Fakes.

PHILO: Don't be stupid—the stuff was from my own department.

OTIS: They were fakes, Marin. The Reschev Memorandum was a fake, and so was the Geller business. Blinds, both of them, and that takes us back four months.

PHILO: You're wrong—

OTIS: I'm not wrong because Geller's dead. What do you think I was doing in Vienna when you showed up?

PHILO: (*Shaken*) I didn't know. I swear I didn't know. If they were using me I didn't know it.

OTIS: Then how did you get out?

(PHILO *now understands the implication*.)

PHILO: You think I made a deal with them?

OTIS: I think you might have. A man working from inside my operation . . .

PHILO: You're mad. And they're not stupid. If I had made a deal they'd expect you to think of it.

OTIS: So they shot that poor bastard Comisky.

(PHILO *is shaken by that*.)

PHILO: Oh . . . Otis, if you think that, there's no talking to you.

OTIS: I don't like that shooting. It makes you look too clean for words, it's like a diploma. I don't like it at all. Those babies don't shoot the wrong man, and they don't shoot anybody on a frontier railroad track like it was their nomination for an Oscar. If they wanted you they could have taken you any time you stepped outside your front door. Why didn't they?

PHILO: If you want to know what I think, I think now that they *were* on to me, they found out I'd gone; but they didn't know where I was till I showed my papers on that last train, and then there was no time to do things properly, just a quick bullet at the frontier for the man with the monkey.

OTIS: You'd never have got so far.

PHILO: I was careful, and I had the right papers.

OTIS: You would have been followed for weeks, everywhere. They would have known everything you were doing.

PHILO: How do you know? Maybe I had a tail, maybe not. Maybe I lost him or he lost me. Maybe I was luckier than I knew. I don't know, and you don't know.

OTIS: I didn't know. But there's a doubt, and that's enough. The British don't want you. Do you, Sanders?

(SANDERS *says nothing*.)

PHILO: Now wait a minute—I'm not asking you for a job. But a home is one thing you owe me.

(*He turns to* SANDERS.)

I was your man, I played your game for fifteen years, and now I want to come *home*.

SANDERS: I'm sorry . . . You're a bad risk, that's all. I really am sorry, Marin . . . you know what they're like.

OTIS: They didn't like the Reschev thing going wrong. It cost a lot of money. And they didn't like Geller being dead. I don't like it either. In fact if I had my way, I wouldn't let you walk away quite so fast and easy.

(OTIS *turns to leave the room. On his turn,* PHILO *moves forward in anger to grab him, but* SANDERS *restrains* PHILO; *which saves* PHILO's *life, because* OTIS *has turned back with a gun in his hand. This tableau slowly relaxes*.)

PHILO: Yes . . . you really believe it, don't you? You think I came over to work from your factory.

OTIS: I doubt they were hoping for the jackpot, not in the factory but maybe somewhere on the road . . . I guess they'd know I wouldn't employ a Russian national in the factory, however clean he was.

PHILO: (*His worst moment*) *I'm not Russian!*

(*Even* OTIS *is taken aback by that*.)

OTIS: Like you said, look at the maps.

(OTIS *goes out*.)

50. INT. SANDER'S OFFICE. DAY

From a zip-bag, SANDERS *is taking out the possessions which had been taken from* PHILO *on his arrival*.

PHILO *watches him from the chair, his energy gone*.

SANDERS: Wallet . . . money . . . diary . . . lighter.

(*The lighter is in pieces.* SANDERS *reassembles it*.)

PHILO: You're making a mistake.

SANDERS: It's like this, Marin. There are two kinds of mistake Otis can make. He can let a bad apple in or keep a good apple out. If he makes the first mistake things could go very badly for Otis. If he makes the second mistake—well, who's going to ever know?

(*Hands over the lighter.*)

Lighter.

(*Opens a cigarette case.*)

How many cigarettes did you have in here.

PHILO: I don't know.

(SANDERS *reaches into his pocket for his own case and feeds a few of his cigarettes into Philo's case.*)

SANDERS: The Americans are so touching. They still expect to find something inside a cigarette.

PHILO: Where am I supposed to go?

SANDERS: That's up to you. Anywhere they'll have you. Shop around.

PHILO: Shop? I can't even move. I've got to have papers—you know that.

SANDERS: I could mention a couple of embassies to you. It's most unfortunate. There used to be quite a few places, but nowadays it's all one big place, underneath.

(PHILO *stares out of the window.*)

PHILO: They'll be looking for me. I think you know that, Sanders.

SANDERS: (*Evenly*) If they find you I'll know it. It really isn't my show, you know.

PHILO: Sanders, I'll tell you this now. Otis is going to be looking for me himself. Perhaps next month, perhaps next year—it could be longer; but that Reschev paper was the real thing, and when Otis realizes that, he's going to need me *badly*. He's going to need me to save his little war, *and* his career. But you tell him not to waste his time, because now I wouldn't *spit* on him, not if he was on *fire*.

51. INT. PHILO'S ROOM. NIGHT

PHILO, *drinking, alone, lying on the bed.*

He hears sounds outside the window and goes to look. In the yard, a horse is pulling the Fiat in, with the BOY *at the horse's head, and* ACHERSON *at the wheel.* ACHERSON *gets out of the car, and looks up steadily at* PHILO *while* PHILO *stares back.*

52. INT. SECOND (ACHERSONS') ROOM. CONTINUATION
CAROL *also watching from the window.*
This room is bare . . . two beds, a couple of chairs, a washstand.

53. INT. HOTEL CORRIDOR. NIGHT
The DESK CLERK *leads* LAUREL *and* HARDY *to one of the bedroom doors. He knocks. The door is opened by a wild-looking middle-aged woman with a parrot on her shoulder.*
WOMAN: What is it, Joseph?
JOSEPH: There are some men, they wish to speak with you.
      (LAUREL *and* HARDY *move in politely but firmly.*)

54. INT. WOMAN'S ROOM. CONTINUATION
The room is a menagerie of pets of all kinds, and consequently squalid.
WOMAN: The maid refuses to clean my room, Joseph. Will you
      speak to her?
HARDY: We are friends of Mr Kramer.
CLERK: You remember Mr Kramer? With the monkey?
WOMAN: Of course. I have not seen him since he left here.
CLERK: These men were wondering if you knew . . . if he told
      you where he was going.
WOMAN: He was my friend.
HARDY: Naturally.
WOMAN: As you see I have many friends, but he was unique, you
      understand.
LAUREL: I understand. He talked to you.
WOMAN: All my friends talk to me.
LAUREL: Oh yes. (*To parrot*) Where's Kramer?
      (*He tries to ruffle the parrot's neck and gets nipped.* LAUREL *looks around.*)
      Which is your best friend?
WOMAN: (*Indicating parrot*) My oldest friend is Tamburlaine. He
      is very old.
LAUREL: Yes . . . well . . . here's a friend.
      (LAUREL *strokes a puppy, making friends.*)
HARDY: About Mr Kramer. Is he in town?
WOMAN: No, in the country.
HARDY: In the country? Where?

WOMAN: It's a secret.

HARDY: A secret? We're his friends.

WOMAN: That's what he said. He said you'll come and say you are his friends.

(LAUREL *produces a wicked looking flick-knife and snaps the blade out, with his other hand holding up the puppy by the scruff of its neck. The* WOMAN *and the* CLERK *stare at him in disbelief.* LAUREL *smiles.*)

HARDY: I'm sorry about my friend. Now, for one dog—where is Mr Kramer?

55. INT. ACHERSON'S ROOM. NIGHT

ACHERSON *and* CAROL *are lying on their backs on separate beds, not talking, perhaps smoking. Faint music is heard—a local band.*

ACHERSON: Well, here we are.

CAROL: Here we are.

ACHERSON: Boris says that Stanislavsky the welder will be brought from Zlens in the morning.

CAROL: How big is that hole?

(ACHERSON *makes a small hole with his finger and thumb.*)

Did nobody think of chewing-gum?

ACHERSON: Stanislavsky works with nothing else. It's his method.

CAROL: (*Amiably*) Oh, shut up.

ACHERSON: (*Pause.*) Well, I think I'll get drunk, then.

(*A knock at the door.*)

CAROL: Yes, why don't you? Come in!

(PHILO *enters.*)

PHILO: Excuse me.

CAROL: Hello, Mr Kramer. Thank you for arranging the room.

PHILO: I'm afraid it is not very nice, but of course they are not used to . . .

CAROL: Of course.

PHILO: (*Pause.*) I've been thinking about . . . about you being here.

CAROL: Oh yes?

PHILO: (*To* ACHERSON) I see you do not wish to talk to me. I am sorry I was rude to you.

ACHERSON: Not at all. But thank you anyway for the thought.

CAROL: What were you thinking about?

PHILO: About coincidence. I think this is the first time any tourist has spent the night in this village, in this house. Why you?— why now?

CAROL: Funnily enough, my mind was going on the same lines. In fact I was wondering whether Charles had arranged the whole thing.

(ACHERSON *looks at her in sharp surprise.* PHILO *is also taken aback.*)

PHILO: Why should you think that?

CAROL: We were supposed to be having dinner with some people tonight. He doesn't like them.

ACHERSON: (*Relapsing*) Oh, don't be ridiculous.

CAROL: The Fosters will think we've stood them up. They'll be disappointed.

ACHERSON: Giles Foster will be *very* disappointed.

CAROL: And *I'm* disappointed—

(ACHERSON *gets suddenly to his feet.*)

ACHERSON: (*To* PHILO) Come on—I'll buy you a drink. What's that music?

PHILO: The wedding feast. The whole village is there.

ACHERSON: Can we go?

PHILO: You will be welcomed. There is a tradition of hospitality here.

ACHERSON: Good. (*To* CAROL) Coming?

CAROL: No, thanks.

(ACHERSON *hesitates, and then leaves with* PHILO.)

56. INT. OUTSIDE ACHERSONS' ROOM. CONTINUATION

As they go . . .

PHILO: The Fosters?

ACHERSON: Friends of ours in Monte.

PHILO: The British Consul?

ACHERSON: Yes. I was at school with him. Always was a little toady. Do you know him?

PHILO: No. Is that why you came here?

ACHERSON: No—I told you. A sales trip.

PHILO: Oh yes. Another coincidence. Where did you go last year?

141

ACHERSON: Majorca. I think I mentioned that too.

PHILO: And before that?

ACHERSON: Italy. No—that was the year before. Paris last year. Wonderful town but the French are awful, the waiters and so on, they're tip mad. No place like home, is there?

PHILO: When do you go back?

ACHERSON: Tomorrow night. Last train to Trieste then the sleeper to Paris, and the boat train from there . . . Ever been to England?

PHILO: Yes. Years ago.

ACHERSON: Well, if you ever think of going back I hope you'll look us up. We're in the book. Acherson. Will you remember?

PHILO: I'll remember Toytown International.

ACHERSON: I doubt that you'll find me there, between you and me. Carol doesn't know it yet but I'm sort of due for the push.

PHILO: Oh. I'm sorry. Why?

ACHERSON: Long story. I'm not really their type.

57. INT./EXT. WEDDING FEAST. NIGHT

Whatever this involves, it involves music, dancing and drinking not to say drunkenness.

Judging by ACHERSON'*s state, a good lot of drinking time has elapsed.*

PHILO, *also drunker but joylessly, finds* ACHERSON, *among new friends. They are able to speak English,* ACHERSON *and* PHILO, *without being understood by those around them.*

ACHERSON: Frightfully good party, old man. I wish Carol would come down.

PHILO: Yes—she could take pictures.

ACHERSON: (*Hush-hush*) Natives don't like it—ruined her last film, she says. I say, you don't happen to have a ladies' nightie and some perfumed soap . . . ?

PHILO: I'm afraid not.

ACHERSON: She wanted to get away from the tourists. Now she wants perfumed soap. Never mind, let's have a drink.

PHILO: I like your wife very much. You don't mind me saying that?

ACHERSON: Not at all, old man.

PHILO: How long have you been married?

ACHERSON: Four years. It's the only life, you know. Splendid girl, Carol. Didn't want to marry me at first.

PHILO: No?

ACHERSON: No, stuck on a tennis champion. Thick as two planks.

PHILO: Do you play tennis?

ACHERSON: Golf. Handicap of eighty-one. Play much golf?

PHILO: Not much.

ACHERSON: You should. If you played golf you'd know people. (*Pauses.*) Still, I don't suppose there's a lot of golf around here.

PHILO: Not a lot.

ACHERSON: (*Nodding wisely*) They haven't got the grass.

PHILO: What else do you do?

ACHERSON: How do you mean—?

PHILO: I want to know about your life.

ACHERSON: Oh, it's a good life, on the whole—lots of friends, bridge friends, golf friends . . . I don't know . . . I mow the lawn and help with the dishes. Quiet life, really, I don't ask for more. Of course, England is the place, isn't it? I mean, if you're English. God, I must sound—sorry, sorry, old man, where was I?—No, The thing about England is the *trees*. Don't you agree?

PHILO: The trees?

ACHERSON: You don't get nice trees in other places, not the variety. Nice trees are taken for granted in England. Yes, awfully fond of trees, damned fond, I don't mind telling you; I say, I'm not drunk, you know, not entirely. Carol's got a tree, you know—her own. I actually *bought* her a tree for her birthday. You can do that—phone them up and tell them to send round a tree, and round it comes, on a lorry, not a sapling, a *tree*. They dig a hole and in it goes, bingo. Cherry tree. No cherries, it's the blossom she likes. I'd do almost anything for Carol.

(*He wipes away a tear.*)

PHILO: Yes. I hope you will be happy, and find a job where you— where you are their type. It's not good, is it, if you're not really interested in the things.

ACHERSON: What things?

PHILO: Well, the toys, of course.

ACHERSON: Oh ah. The toys.

(*He starts to giggle.*)

PHILO: What's the matter?

ACHERSON: Oh, the whole thing's so frightful, old man. I'm glad
I'm going really.

PHILO: Why are they throwing you out?

ACHERSON: I stopped a few black marks, that's all. That's what
the factory is all about. The actual job is merely the surface
activity. Underneath that runs the main current of
preoccupation, which is keeping one's nose clean at all times.
This means that when things go wrong you have to pass the
blame along the line, like pass-the-parcel, till the music
stops—and you don't know the half of it.

PHILO: No?

ACHERSON: No. I have the title of Co-ordinator. The lowest rank
of technical responsibility. Do you see the hideous subtlety of
that position. All the black marks at the bottom rise like
damp till they reach me. And those that start at the top are
deflected down. I am a sort of elephants' graveyard for every
black mark somewhere in motion in the Department.

(*He looks earnestly at* PHILO, *caution apparently gone.*)

They're making a scapegoat out of me, old man. Acherson
pays so that honour is satisfied, and the big chief can carry
on. Well, he's probably right. And furthermore I don't care
because it was making me sick—the callous abstraction of
human lives: the pin moved across the map, the card
removed from the index . . . it's a trick, old man, a sleight of
mind which allows the occasional squalid alliance for the
necessary end, the exceptional act of injustice for the overall
good, the regrettable sacrifice for the majority's health—yes,
he's probably right and he's certainly got the cleanest nose in
Christendom but if there's a God above it will all catch up on
him one day and perhaps even he will see himself as the cold-
blooded zombie he really is, and I wish to God I could be
there.

(*It is evident that, in his cups,* ACHERSON *has gone beyond the*

144

physical presence of PHILO; *but seeing* PHILO *staring at him,*
ACHERSON *registers the shock of self-awareness—and tries to*
smile, but PHILO *can't resist it now—he comes clean.*)
PHILO: Otis . . .

(ACHERSON'*s brain takes this in. He tries to say something but his*
instinct is to get away from his own indiscretion; he staggers
away, starts to run, with PHILO *going after him, leaving the party*
music, etc.)

58. EXT. VILLAGE. NIGHT/DAWN. CONTINUATION

The street is deserted. ACHERSON *stumbles and runs into an open space*
where there is a fountain pool or a horse trough; at which point PHILO
catches up with him, grabs him, and pushes him under the water.
ACHERSON *comes up fighting and spluttering, and goes down again*
under the water. PHILO *drags him up and shakes him, and lets him go.*
The whole experience—and the water—have done something to sober
both of them.

PHILO: Now you tell me why you are in Montebianca.
ACHERSON: Who are you?
PHILO: Marin.
ACHERSON: Marin?
PHILO: Philo.
ACHERSON: Philo Marin?
PHILO: No. My code name was Philo.
ACHERSON: Code name? I'm afraid I don't know what you're
   talking about.
PHILO: Well, I'm not talking about toy trains.
   (*After a pause* ACHERSON *gives up.*)
ACHERSON: You see how I'm not their type.
PHILO: You remember Philo?
ACHERSON: Yes . . . I remember when you came out. There was a
   fuss, wasn't there?—at the frontier . . . Small world.
PHILO: Is it? What's this so-called sales trip you've told your wife
   about?
ACHERSON: It's just a security leak at the Consulate. They think
   the place has sprung a leak.
PHILO: A coincidence, you mean?
ACHERSON: That's right . . . What the hell would I want with you?

(*He picks himself up, his clothes dripping.*)

PHILO: What do they say about me? Or am I forgotten?

ACHERSON: No, you're remembered.

PHILO: What is remembered? What do they say? That I was a traitor?

ACHERSON: (*Uncomfortably*) Well, I wouldn't call it that. You were one of them, weren't you? Doesn't that make you a patriot?

PHILO: Acherson, you're a *pig*.

ACHERSON: (*Turning to go*) Well, there's no point in discussing it. It was a long time ago—and I'm getting pneumonia.

PHILO: No—I want you to know what happened.

ACHERSON: You were blown, weren't you?

PHILO: I don't know if I was or not. But Otis thought they'd let me out on a long string.

ACHERSON: Otis would.

PHILO: Yes, of course he would, he'd be in the wrong job if he didn't—but you're as bad as Otis, Acherson—worse because you're not even honest. You get a little drunk and you start moralizing and you think because you have seen through the dirt, that makes you clean. But you didn't have the morality to get out before you were kicked out, and to tell Otis why.

ACHERSON: Point taken. Now if you'd excuse me . . .

PHILO: I'm sorry Acherson, but I won't excuse you. You talk about Otis making lives into abstract bits of his game—but I stand in front of you and my life means nothing. Otis knows what he did to me, but you don't know, Acherson. You think I'm lucky not to be in a British gaol or a Russian cemetery, so on the whole I'm OK.

ACHERSON: No . . . that's not . . .

PHILO: You don't know what it is to be an outlaw. There are only two sides in Europe now and I'm tainted to both. Well, I found a place, and here I rot—in this no man's land among people who don't speak my language, where the landscape, the smells, the architecture, the very air, is foreign to me. You come here for a few days and you think it's charming till you have to spend one night too close to it, and then you'll go back home and tell your golf friends about your little

146

adventure. Well, tell them about me, Acherson. Tell them
what they did to me.
(PHILO *has followed* ACHERSON *towards the bar, which is dark
and empty.* ACHERSON *turns before going in.*)

ACHERSON: Look, I'll talk to Otis—

PHILO: Don't waste your time.

ACHERSON: No, no, I'll tell him . . .

PHILO: You don't understand, Acherson. He had his chance. I'd
rather die in this prison.

59. INT. ACHERSON'S ROOM. CONTINUATION

Dawn. CAROL *is asleep.* ACHERSON *comes in quietly. He starts to strip
off his wet clothes, and to dry himself.* CAROL *wakes.*

CAROL: Charles . . . !

ACHERSON: It's all right. Go back to sleep.

CAROL: What happened to you?

ACHERSON: Our friend pushed me in the fountain.
(CAROL *lies back and chuckles.*)

CAROL: Good party?

ACHERSON: What do you think of him?

CAROL: He doesn't know whether to be friendly or suspicious.
What did he have to say?

ACHERSON: Quite a bit. People like that . . . what does one do
about them?
(*The note in his voice brings her up.*)

CAROL: He upset you.

ACHERSON: He did a bit.

CAROL: You're sorry for him?

ACHERSON: I suppose so.

CAROL: You can't afford to be sorry for people. Not if there's
nothing you can do about it.

ACHERSON: He'd like to leave. I offered to put in a word for him at
home, but he didn't go for that.

CAROL: Oh . . . perhaps he'll change his mind.

ACHERSON: He doesn't like us.

CAROL: He likes me. Let's not talk about him.
(*She comes over to his bed, wearing only underwear, and kisses
him tamely.*)

It's better than the hotel now.

ACHERSON: Is it?

CAROL: More sordid.

(*She kisses him again.*) Much better.

(*He starts to respond.*)

60. EXT. THE ROAD. EARLY MORNING

Along the unmade road, out of sight of the village, a handful of
CHILDREN *are walking, fooling around as they go. They are dressed*
for school and carry books. The BOY *is among them.*

Their road is approaching a more important metalled road. There are
still no houses in view.

The group reaches the junction. A car is heard approaching.

The car arrives, slows down.

HARDY *is driving,* LAUREL *is looking at a map. They are going to turn*
into the village road but they are not certain about it. The car stops
some way from the CHILDREN.

The BOY *looks at the car, at* LAUREL *and* HARDY, *and he feels that*
these are the 'debt collectors'. He goes up to the car.

LAUREL: Ah . . . Ask him.

HARDY: (*To* BOY) Vlastok? (*He points.*)

(*The* BOY *shakes his head. He points down the main road, and*
signifies a turn further along.)

BOY: Vlastok—that way—the next road.

(LAUREL *squints at his map, but* HARDY *is already reversing the*
car. They drive off in the direction indicated by the BOY.
A tattered old bus that serves as a school bus arrives. The other
children climb aboard, but the BOY *breaks away and starts to trot*
back towards the village.)

61. EXT. BAR. THE YARD. MORNING

STANISLAVSKY *the welder is busy welding under the Fiat.* ACHERSON
stands by.

62. INT. ACHERSON'S ROOM. CONTINUATION

The door is open. CAROL, *dressed, is repairing her face and hair.*
PHILO *comes to the door.*

CAROL: Hello. Charles has just gone down.

PHILO: Is the car all right?

CAROL: Pretty well. He's just checking it. You look a bit rough.

PHILO: Yes. I'm sorry I kept your husband up so late . . . I think he's a good man.

CAROL: Well, why shouldn't he be a good man?

(CAROL *takes some Alka Seltzer out of her handbag.*)

Here's something for you. Charles had some.

(*There is water in a jug, and a glass.*)

I suppose the water's all right?

PHILO: Oh yes—much better than you drink in London.

CAROL: Sorry.

(*She gives him the drink.*)

PHILO: Thank you.

CAROL: Who looks after you?

PHILO: I don't need much looking after. I eat downstairs on credit. I've got a bank account in town.

CAROL: Do you go?

PHILO: No. It's a three-mile walk to the bus. Boris usually goes in for me, if I need anything.

CAROL: You're a bit of a mystery, aren't you?

PHILO: I do not think so. A refugee drinking up his savings. There must be many. Do you mind if I ask you a pointless question?

CAROL: No, go ahead. I don't promise to answer.

PHILO: What kind of trees do you have in your garden at home?

CAROL: Trees?

PHILO: Yes.

CAROL: (*Amused*) Well, let's see—there are only three I think, a couple of elms or something like that, and a cherry.

PHILO: Thank you.

CAROL: Is that all?

PHILO: Yes. Do you like cherries?

CAROL: Yes, but there's no fruit on it, just flowers.

PHILO: Ah. Does your husband look after the garden?

CAROL: What, him? Golf most weekends.

PHILO: Do you play?

CAROL: No.

PHILO: What do you play?

CAROL: Nothing.

PHILO: You never did?

CAROL: I played some tennis—look, what is this?

PHILO: I'm sorry. Mrs Acherson, I'm very glad you came this way. You are an innocent person.

CAROL: That sounds rather dull.

PHILO: Oh no, innocence is rare.

CAROL: Mr Kramer . . . are you in some kind of trouble?

PHILO: (*Pause*.) I'd like to ask your husband a favour.

CAROL: Oh. You won't get *him* into trouble, will you?

PHILO: No.

CAROL: All right. I'll be down in a couple of minutes.

63. EXT. THE YARD. MORNING

ACHERSON *is coming out from under the car*. BORIS *finishes pouring in petrol from a can; he screws on the cap*. STANISLAVSKY *has a tiny Citroën, battered; he packs his tools*.

PHILO *helps* ACHERSON *to his feet*.

PHILO: Is it all right?

ACHERSON: Yes.

PHILO: Leaving now?

ACHERSON: In a few minutes.

PHILO: About last night.

ACHERSON: I behaved stupidly.

PHILO: Yes. But you're all right. (*Pause*.) You said you might help me.

ACHERSON: If I can.

PHILO: You can. I'd like to come with you. Give me a few minutes—I haven't got much I want to take.

ACHERSON: Hold on, old man—go where?

PHILO: I want to come with you, when you leave the country.

ACHERSON: What do you mean?

PHILO: I want to travel with you. Party of three. Tourists. Friends.

ACHERSON: To England?

PHILO: No, only as far as Trieste.

ACHERSON: (*Bewildered*) You want to go to Trieste?

PHILO: I want to go home. I can make my own way from Trieste.

ACHERSON: I don't understand—what do you want?

PHILO: (*Climbing*) Papers, Acherson. I'm asking you for papers. And for your company over the border. Three English tourists. They aren't going to pick me out.

ACHERSON: (*Up*) What the hell are you talking about?

PHILO: *Papers*, Acherson! British papers! I've earned them. I'm *owed* them. Now I'm asking you to give them to me.

ACHERSON: How on earth do you expect me to—

PHILO: Don't lie to me, Acherson. Refuse if you're afraid of Otis, but don't lie to me. I know you've got the rank, and I know Foster has got the blank documents. Every season some British tourist loses his passport, and I know what papers Foster has got. They just need his stamp.
(*Pause.*) Look, I can't leave the country in my own identity because the West doesn't want me, I tried before. And I can't go East because the Russians *do* want me. But as a British subject I can get into Trieste, and from Trieste I can disappear. I've still got friends, and I want to go home.

ACHERSON: You don't know what you're asking.

PHILO: Yes, I do. I'm asking you to deny the Otises. I'm a used-up spy without a country, and I'm asking you to recognize me.

ACHERSON: Look, I can probably fix a British visa, given time, but that's for England, Marin. You can't use it like a free pass to the world.

PHILO: I don't want to go to England. I'm dying, Acherson, I'm slowly killing myself, bottle by bottle. Well, it doesn't matter very much, but I don't want to die here, I want to die where I was born. I might last years, or only weeks or I could get caught on my first day, but I want that day, Acherson.
(CAROL *comes prettily towards the car.*)

CAROL: Have you paid?

ACHERSON: Yes.

CAROL: Well, I suppose we should . . . . (*To* PHILO) Thank you for everything.

ACHERSON: (*Like a sudden decision*) Mr Kramer is coming with us.

CAROL: Oh—fine. Into town?

PHILO: I hope to travel with you when you leave.

CAROL: Oh really? A holiday in England?

PHILO: Just as far as Trieste. Your friend Mr Foster is going to help with the papers. That was the favour.

CAROL: I'm sure Giles will do all he can to help. If he won't do it for Charles, he'll do it for me.

(*She glances at* ACHERSON.)

He thinks I fancy him, but I don't.

(*She gives* ACHERSON *a brief kiss.*)

ACHERSON: All right, let's get a move on.

64. EXT. THE ROAD. DAY

Long shot.

The Fiat is going back along the road.

The BOY *is short-cutting to the village, over the hill. He sees the car in the distance, and pauses to watch it then continues to hurry.*

65. INT. FIAT. DAY

ACHERSON *driving,* CAROL *in front,* PHILO *at the back amid luggage and boxes of toys—guns, cars, etc.* PHILO *holds the monkey.*

PHILO: Will you do something for me?

ACHERSON: What's that?

PHILO: We go through Pilz—the next village on the main road. Can you stop at the school there. I want to say goodbye to the boy. It won't take a minute.

ACHERSON: Yes, all right.

(*Another car is coming towards them—the* LAUREL *and* HARDY *car, say a Mercedes. The road is narrow and the Mercedes is travelling fast.*

An accident is avoided.)

Who's that?

PHILO: (*Worried*) I don't know.

66. EXT. VILLAGE. CONTINUATION

The BOY *runs into the village, worried and scared.*

The Mercedes is already there, parked, empty.

The BOY *runs straight into the bar.*

67. INT. PHILO'S ROOM. CONTINUATION
LAUREL *and* HARDY *are quietly looking at the room. They realize that*
the bird has flown.
The BOY *is heard running. He arrives in the room.*
The BOY *stops dead.* LAUREL *and* HARDY *recognize him.* HARDY *sighs*
and looks at LAUREL.
The BOY *backs away, but* LAUREL *closes the door. The* BOY *is really*
frightened and starts to cry. HARDY *opens the door with a sudden*
movement and goes. LAUREL *follows him.*

68. EXT. VILLAGE. CONTINUATION
The Mercedes drives away at speed.

69. EXT. THE METALLED ROAD. DAY
The Mercedes at speed.

70. EXT. THE METALLED ROAD. DAY
The Fiat is being driven sedately.

71. EXT. THE METALLED ROAD. DAY
The Mercedes at speed drives through Pilz and out of frame, leaving
the Fiat in frame parked by the school.
PHILO *comes out of the school looking disappointed and puzzled.*

72. EXT. MONTEBIANCA TOWN. DAY
The Fiat drives into town.

73. EXT. MONTEBIANCA HOTEL. CONTINUATION
The Fiat stops to drop CAROL *and* PHILO. *They go into the hotel. The*
Fiat moves on.

74. EXT. BRITISH CONSULATE. CONTINUATION
The Fiat stops round the corner. ACHERSON *gets out and walks into the*
Consulate.

75. INT. CONSULATE. CONTINUATION.
ACHERSON *climbs the rather fine staircase.*

76. INT. CONSULATE OFFICE. CONTINUATION
GILES FOSTER *in one chair.*
ACHERSON *enters.*
OTIS *is standing by the window.*
OTIS: Hello, Charles . . . How did it go?
    (ACHERSON *sits tiredly in a chair.*)
ACHERSON: He's at the hotel. I think we've got him all right. But I
    don't think he'll play when he finds out.
        God, what a pantomime, eh, Giles?

77. INT. HOTEL BATHROOM. DAY
PHILO *enjoying a bath. The monkey is there.*

78. INT. HOTEL BATHROOM. DAY
PHILO *shaving, taking off much of his beard.*

79. INT. BARBERSHOP. DAY
PHILO *getting a haircut.*
CAROL *waits for him.*
The Mercedes cruises by slowly. LAUREL *and* HARDY *looking for the
Fiat.*

80. EXT. CLOTHES SHOP. DAY
PHILO *in new clothes, emerging with* CAROL.

81. INT. PHOTOGRAPHER'S. DAY
Flash! PHILO *has his picture taken.*

82. INT. CONSULATE OFFICE. DAY
Close-up of Philo's new photo on document. The document is held by
OTIS. ACHERSON *is the other person in the room.*
OTIS: There you are, Charles. With this he'll be almost as British
    as you are. And that's awfully British . . . old man.
    (ACHERSON, *it is at once clear, is in no mood for jokes, especially
    jokes about Philo.*)
ACHERSON: He really does want to go his own way, you know.
OTIS: That's all right. Just get him on that train.
ACHERSON: What happens when he gets to Trieste?

OTIS: Charles, just get him on the train. The rest is taken care of.

ACHERSON: Have you got a legal hold on him?

OTIS: (*Smiles.*) Well, he'll have British papers, won't he?

ACHERSON: All this to get one old man through one gate. Why are you here? Why do you want him so badly?

OTIS: You were briefed. You were told enough to operate on. What the hell did you expect?

ACHERSON: I expected to be told the truth. He's not *working*. I *know* he isn't. He's got *nothing*. He's drunk a lot of the time and he sees nobody. And what on earth could anyone pick up in this place?

OTIS: Look, you've done your job. So far he trusts you. So just finish it.

ACHERSON: (*Heedless*) But he was clean when he came out . . . You know that now, don't you?
(*It's an accusation.* OTIS *hesitates, but nods, and tells the truth.*)

OTIS: Yes. And he's not working. All right, I dropped him and now we need him. I made a mistake.

ACHERSON: (*Laughs shortly.*) Black mark . . . So here you are, taking an interest.

OTIS: Are you trying to tell me I'm here to save my own skin?

ACHERSON: Are you trying to tell me you aren't?

OTIS: (*Sharply*) Don't push it, Charles. They might junk me yet but they'd still need Marin. And badly. We've got a new pipeline on Reschev. It looked all wrong but now it could make a lot of important sense and we need Marin to read it. *That's* why I'm here, so get off your white horse. It never bothered you much while you sat behind your desk in London—you've got people like Marin walking tightropes all over Eastern Europe and some of them fall off; it never bothered you, and now suddenly it's all become a nice old drunk dreaming of the old country. Well, forget it.
(*Pause.*)
(*Forgiving*) Look, you and I—we've worked pretty well together. I thought we understood each other.

ACHERSON: I'm beginning to understand you, Otis. Do you know, I surprised myself a little, talking to Marin. When I got to the bit about you, what a bastard you were and all that, I surprised myself. I found I was quite articulate on the subject.

OTIS: Feel free. Just deliver.

ACHERSON: Oh yes, I'll deliver. But it won't do you any good. He hates you and he hates us.

OTIS: Yes, he's full of poison. It's had time to build up, and I'll need time to release it. He wants a change of scene, someone to talk to. He'll come round, I know him. Just get him on the train.

ACHERSON: No. He doesn't want to go to England.

OTIS: He thinks he doesn't, but it's just his hurt feelings. England was what he was holding out for.

ACHERSON: It's gone sour on him. You turned it sour. Look, he's not a professional, and you're playing by professional rules. He's a sick old man who probably shortened his life by the number of years he's worked for us and then got kicked out for his pains. You can't make it *good* now.

OTIS: (*Losing patience*) I'm not here to make things good. And nor are you. What the hell do you think I'm running—a compensations board? He was the victim of an accident and he wasn't insured, and it was a pity for him, and you don't like it. Well, *I* don't like it. But he can't go home now because the first time he gets drunk, or the third, or the fortieth, he's going to confide in someone again; and if they find out what it is we've got then what we've got is no *good* any more, do you understand *that*?

ACHERSON: Yes. Yes, I suppose I do.

OTIS: Good. Well, that's why we spent two months looking for him before we got lucky. The Russians have been looking for him for two years. Let's see if we can keep ahead for one more day.

83. EXT. STREET. DAY

The Fiat is where ACHERSON *parked it.*

LAUREL *and* HARDY *have found it.*

LAUREL *stands on the pavement, keeping a watch.*

HARDY *is half in the car.*

84. INT. CAR. CONTINUATION
HARDY *is rummaging around, puzzled at finding boxes of toys. He tosses cars, six-shooters and dolls aside; shakes his head. Must be the wrong Fiat. He opens the glove locker, looks behind the sun-visors, in the door pockets. He gets out of the car.*

85. EXT. STREET. CONTINUATION
HARDY *walks to* LAUREL.
HARDY: I don't know. Toys.
LAUREL: We're wasting time.
HARDY: No . . . It smells right. We'll see.

86. EXT. STREET. DAY
The car waits. LAUREL *and* HARDY *sit in the front seats.*

87. INT. CAR. CONTINUATION
LAUREL *looks straight ahead—cross-cut* LAUREL'*s POV.* HARDY *watches the mirror—cross-cut* HARDY'*s POV.*
A few people approach and pass from each direction. LAUREL *and* HARDY *are looking for someone who hesitates on seeing them.*
HARDY *sees* ACHERSON *in the mirror.* ACHERSON *hesitates, and walks on.*
HARDY: Here he is.
> (ACHERSON *walks past the Fiat, disowning it.*
> LAUREL *and* HARDY *glance at each other and watch as* ACHERSON *walks on ahead.*
> HARDY *starts the car.*
> *Insert* ACHERSON'*s tense face.*)

88. EXT. STREET. CONTINUATION
The Fiat moves forward slowly. When it is a few yards behind ACHERSON, LAUREL *gets out of the Fiat while it is still moving at walking pace. The Fiat overtakes* ACHERSON, *stops.* HARDY *gets out and turns to* ACHERSON *and moves to meet him.*
ACHERSON *looks over his shoulder to see* LAUREL *walking towards him. They move up to* ACHERSON, *and without comment, ignoring* ACHERSON'*s protest, frisk him, taking out his wallet and an envelope first.*

ACHERSON: What the devil—? Who are you?

(*There is nothing in* ACHERSON's *pockets to enlighten* LAUREL *and* HARDY. HARDY *goes through* ACHERSON's *wallet.*)

I don't want any trouble. There's money in there—take it.

(HARDY *drops the money and bits of paper on the ground. He hesitates.* LAUREL *is disgusted.*)

LAUREL: Toy salesman . . .

ACHERSON: That's right.

(HARDY *rips open the envelope. It contains Philo's documents, with the photo.*)

89. EXT. TOWN/COUNTRY. DAY

HARDY *drives the Fiat.* ACHERSON *sits next to him. Behind* ACHERSON *is* LAUREL *with a gun to* ACHERSON's *neck.*

90. EXT. COUNTRY. DAY

The Fiat draws up off the road at a lonely spot. HARDY *gets out and looks around. He nods at* LAUREL.

LAUREL *gets out from the back, opens* ACHERSON's *door and stands a few paces back.* LAUREL *beckons. He holds his gun down, relaxed.*

ACHERSON, *without hurrying, picks up a shiny Lone Ranger six-shooter from the floor between the seats. He levels it at* LAUREL, *cocks the hammer.* LAUREL *blinks in surprise and starts to laugh. He brings his gun hand up, but* ACHERSON *fires and the bullet knocks* LAUREL *over backwards.*

HARDY *starts getting his own gun out but* ACHERSON *kills him with his second shot.*

91. INT. RAILWAY STATION. EVENING

This is the station where we saw LAUREL *and* HARDY *arrive.*

A PORTER *trundles the Achersons' luggage.* CAROL *is there. She tips the* PORTER. *The* PORTER *puts the luggage on the platform.*

The train is arriving.

92. INT. STATION BAR. CONTINUATION

ACHERSON *and* PHILO *at a table with drinks. The monkey is in* PHILO's *pocket.* ACHERSON *takes the (ripped) envelope out of his pocket and gives it to* PHILO.

ACHERSON: Marin . . . are you listening to me?

PHILO: What?

ACHERSON: Change your mind. Come all the way.

(PHILO *looks up from examining the papers.*)

PHILO: Why? Why does it matter to you?

ACHERSON: They'll find you and kill you.

PHILO: If they want to kill me badly enough they'll find me in England. I'd rather go home.

ACHERSON: England was your home once.

PHILO: I thought so too but I was wrong.

ACHERSON: (*Almost angry*) Marin—will you listen—

PHILO: What's the matter?—You haven't changed your mind?

ACHERSON: No . . .

PHILO: You don't have to worry about me. Everything's going to be all right.

ACHERSON: That's bloody nonsense!—you're as good as dead if you don't come with me. Please stop thinking about going home—will you, Marin?

PHILO: You don't understand, Acherson . . . I'm old . . . I accept things . . . I think differently. My memories are good ones now. I don't think about the commissars, the fear, the system, all the things that changed when the Russians came. The things I remember don't change. I was born in a small town. I lived in a street which led into a small square and twice a week there was a market in the square. And round about six o'clock in the evening, when the market was packing up, the ground would be littered with vegetables which hadn't sold and were too cheap to save—cabbage leaves, carrots, some peppers. I particularly remember the peppers lying around the edges of the square—red, orange, yellow, green, and all shades in between, all sunset and forest colours, lying about the square. What mattered to us then was that they were edible, and free, but what I remember now is the way the square looked on a summer evening after the market. (*Pause.*) That's what you are giving back to me. (*The train is heard arriving in the station. The few people in the bar get up to leave.* PHILO *stands up.* ACHERSON *sits tense and anguished.*

CAROL *comes into the bar.*)

CAROL: Come on, we must get on the train. The porter's taken the luggage.

(*She turns to leave again, and* PHILO *follows her. The door closes behind them.* ACHERSON *stands up and with a sudden decision moves briskly out, on to the platform, where* PHILO *and* CAROL *are moving away from him.*)

93. THE PLATFORM. CONTINUATION

ACHERSON: (*Shouts*) Marin!

(PHILO *and* CAROL *turn to him.*)

You're not going home!

PHILO: What?

ACHERSON: Forget all that! Otis is on that train.

(PHILO *moves towards him.* CAROL *stares at* ACHERSON, *then turns and starts running towards the train, out of the scene.* PHILO *reaches* ACHERSON.)

The whole thing is his operation. I'm sorry . . .

(PHILO *spits in his face.*)

Marin—please understand—

PHILO: You Judas!

I spit on you. I am ashamed of the stupid old man I am—but on you I *spit*!

ACHERSON: I'm sorry.

PHILO: —because you cheat so much for such a small prize. Well, I will not go with you to England.

ACHERSON: Yes, I know that.

PHILO: You can take away my hope but you will not take my honour.

(PHILO *is raving.* ACHERSON *seems stunned, but now he's suddenly had enough, and he turns angrily on* PHILO.)

ACHERSON: Honour?—what *honour*? You're a stubborn, bitter old man. I don't blame you—it's understandable, you have been ill-used. Otis made a mistake and you paid for it because in the game we're playing his skin is worth more than yours and there's never enough justice to go round. But you carry your grievance around like a badge—that's all your bloody honour is and you've got to like it.

PHILO: I trusted you after I'd forgotten how to trust.

(*The steam goes out of* ACHERSON.)

ACHERSON: It's not such a significant betrayal, judged by the scale of the world's duplicity.

(PHILO *pushes the papers back to* ACHERSON.)

PHILO: I thought you were my friend.

ACHERSON: Well, as it turns out, you were right.

(ACHERSON *pushes the papers back again.*)

I should hang on to these, because you can't stay here. We got to you only just in time, one move ahead of your other friends. If I were you I should take the morning train and see how far you can get.

PHILO: You're lying. Where are they?

ACHERSON: I had to kill them, but there'll be others.

PHILO: (*Incredulous*) You? (*Laughs.*) You can't stop trying, Acherson.

(PHILO *turns to go.*

OTIS *enters the scene.* CAROL *is behind him.* OTIS *greets* PHILO *like an old friend.*)

OTIS: Marin! How are you?

PHILO: I am very much as you last saw me. Please do not waste time in persuasion. Use force or let me go.

OTIS: Marin, I need you.

PHILO: I am the same man, the same risk.

OTIS: Marin . . .

PHILO: No. You had no time for me then and you will not make use of me now.

OTIS: You need me.

PHILO: No. You cheated me, Otis.

OTIS: (*Getting angry*) You're cheating yourself. You want freedom—I'm giving it to you. You want a country—you can have it. You want apologies—you'll get them. But you won't forgive and you won't accept, and I knew you wouldn't so we had to go through this whole bloody charade. And now you want to go home. All right—but first ask yourself to which side you really belong.

PHILO: Not yours, Otis. Not anyone's.

OTIS: Look, there are no neutral corners in this world, not for you. I made a mistake and I'm sorry, but in this world, you are with *us*.

PHILO: Words.

OTIS: You'd rather wait till their triggermen find you?

PHILO: Yes, I would.

(OTIS *pauses, then nods with finality. He turns to* ACHERSON *expressionlessly.*)

OTIS: Are you coming?

ACHERSON: Yes.

OTIS: Think about it, Acherson.

ACHERSON: You can do what you like with me. I've just had enough of this picnic. And at bottom I think you're wrong.

OTIS: You had a duty.

ACHERSON: Duty! He's been conned all down the line. The Russians conned him out of his country, and the British conned him into working for them, and you conned him out of his due at the end of that, and now you're conning him to get what's left and cover up your mistakes. So don't preach at me about duty.

(CAROL *is frightened by this outburst.*)

CAROL: (*Coming forward*) Charles—

ACHERSON: You go ahead. I'll be coming.

CAROL: It's stupid. It may be right but it's stupid.

ACHERSON: Yes, that's about it.

(*The train makes sounds of getting ready to go.*)

OTIS: Come on, let's forget it.

(OTIS *turns to go to the train.* CAROL *turns to follow him.* PHILO *grabs her sleeve.*)

PHILO: You're his *wife*!

(*She looks at him with stone eyes.*)

CAROL: No. No, I'm not, actually.

(*She follows* OTIS. PHILO *is stunned.*)

PHILO: So much deception. Was it all necessary?

ACHERSON: Why not? It was Carol who got through your distrust, wasn't it?

(*He moves.*)

PHILO: Are you really going back?

ACHERSON: Yes.

PHILO: What will they do to you?

ACHERSON: I don't know.

PHILO: Are you frightened?

ACHERSON: No, I'm just tired. Goodbye, Marin.

PHILO: Do you think I'm worth it, Acherson?

ACHERSON: Yes, I think so.

PHILO: (*A curse*) Otis . . . I'll kill him!

(ACHERSON *smiles helplessly and moves.* PHILO *moves with him.*)
You touched me, Acherson. Yes, I am a stubborn, bitter
man, and you *are* stupid, but we are holding out for
something. Aren't we? Stay.

ACHERSON: How can I? What for?

PHILO: They'll break you for this.

ACHERSON: One of those things.

PHILO: (*Bursts out*) You think I'll go with you, don't you?—to
save your neck.

ACHERSON: No. Goodbye.

PHILO: You're blackmailing me!
(*Desperate*) Otis set this up, didn't he?

ACHERSON: No.

PHILO: Tell me he set it up!

ACHERSON: (*Rounds on him.*) That's what you want to think so you
can forget all about it. Well, think it.

PHILO: No—just tell me the truth.

ACHERSON: Otis didn't set it up.

(ACHERSON *starts running towards the train.* PHILO *stands still for
a moment.*)

PHILO: (*Screams*) Acherson!

(PHILO *runs after* ACHERSON *as the train starts to move.*)

94. EXT. TRAIN AT SPEED. NIGHT

95. INT. TRAIN. NIGHT

ACHERSON *stands in the corridor looking out at the night. Behind him
are the closed doors of the sleeping compartment.*

The nearest door opens and OTIS *comes to* ACHERSON'S *shoulder.* PHILO
can be seen sitting inside the compartment, on the bunk.

The adjacent compartment is seen, CAROL *in the doorway.*

OTIS *pats* ACHERSON *on the shoulder.*

OTIS: Very nice. Very nice. (*Pause.*) You need a holiday, Charles.

(OTIS *goes back into the sleeper he shares with* PHILO *and closes the door.*
CAROL *looks at* ACHERSON, *troubled and sympathetic.*)
CAROL: Are you coming in?
(ACHERSON *does not respond, but continues to stare at the black country rushing by.*
Fade to black.)

A Separate Peace

A Play for Television

Characters

JOHN BROWN
NURSE
DOCTOR
NURSE MAGGIE COATES
MATRON
NURSE JONES

SCENE 1

The office of the Beechwood Nursing Home. Behind the reception counter sits a uniformed nurse. It is 2.30 am. A car pulls up outside. JOHN BROWN *enters. He is a biggish man, with a well-lined face: calm, pleasant. He is wearing a nondescript suit and overcoat, and carrying two zipped travelling bags. Looking around, he notes the neatness, the quiet, the flowers, the nice nurse, and is quietly pleased.*

BROWN: Very nice.

NURSE: Good evening . . .

BROWN: 'Evening. A lovely night. Morning.

NURSE: Yes . . . Mr . . . ?

BROWN: I'm sorry to be so late.

NURSE: (Shuffling papers) Were you expected earlier?

BROWN: No. I telephoned.

NURSE: Yes?

BROWN: Yes. You have a room for Mr Brown.

NURSE: Oh!—Have you brought him?

BROWN: I brought myself. Got a taxi by the station. I telephoned from there.

NURSE: You said it was an emergency.

BROWN: That's right. Do you know what time it is?

NURSE: It's half-past two.

BROWN: That's right. An emergency.

NURSE: (*Aggrieved*) I woke the house doctor.

BROWN: A kind thought. But it's all right. Do you want me to sign in?

NURSE: What is the nature of your emergency, Mr Brown?

BROWN: I need a place to stay.

NURSE: Are you ill?

BROWN: No.

167

NURSE: But this is a private hospital . . .

(BROWN *smiles for the first time.*)

BROWN: The best kind. What is a hospital without privacy? It's the privacy I'm after—that and the clean linen . . . (*A thought strikes him.*) I've got money.

NURSE: . . . . the Beechwood Nursing Home.

BROWN: I require nursing. I need to be nursed for a bit. Yes. Where do I sign?

NURSE: I'm sorry, but admissions have to be arranged in advance except in the case of a genuine emergency—I have no authority—

BROWN: What do you want with authority? A nice person like you. (*Moves.*) Where have you put me?

NURSE: (*Moves with him.*) And *you* have no authority—

BROWN: (*Halts.*) That's true. That's one thing I've never had. (*He looks at her flatly.*) I've come a long way.

NURSE: (*Wary*) Would you wait for just one moment?

BROWN: (*Relaxes.*) Certainly. Have you got a sign-in-book? Must abide by the regulations. Should I pay in advance?

NURSE: No, that's quite all right.

BROWN: I've got it—I've got it all in here—

(*He starts trying to open one of the zipped cases, it jams and he hurts his finger. He recoils sharply and puts his finger in his mouth. The* DOCTOR *arrives, dishevelled from being roused.*)

NURSE: Doctor—this is Mr Brown.

DOCTOR: Good evening. What seems to be the trouble?

BROWN: Caught my finger.

DOCTOR: May I see?

(BROWN *holds out his finger: The* DOCTOR *studies it, looks up.*)

DOCTOR: (*Guardedly*) Have you come far?

BROWN: Yes. I've been travelling all day.

(*The* DOCTOR *glances at the* NURSE.)

Not with my finger. I did that just now. Zip stuck.

DOCTOR: Oh. And what—er—

NURSE: Mr Brown says there's nothing wrong with him.

BROWN: That's right—I—

NURSE: He just wants a bed.

BROWN: A room.

DOCTOR: But this isn't a hotel.

BROWN: Exactly.

DOCTOR: Exactly what?

BROWN: I don't follow you.

DOCTOR: Perhaps I'm confused. You see, I was asleep.

BROWN: It's all right. I understand. Well, if someone would show me to my room, I shan't disturb you any further.

DOCTOR: (*With a glance at the* NURSE) I don't believe we have any rooms free at the moment.

BROWN: Oh yes, this young lady arranged it.

NURSE: He telephoned from the station. He said it was an emergency.

DOCTOR: But you've come to the wrong place.

BROWN: No, this is the place all right. What's the matter?

DOCTOR: (*Pause.*) Nothing—nothing's the matter. (*He nods at the* NURSE.) All right.

NURSE: Yes, doctor. (*Murmurs worriedly*) I'll have to make an entry . . .

DOCTOR: Observation.

BROWN: (*Cheerfully*) I'm not much to look at.

NURSE: Let me take those for you, Mr Brown. (*The cases.*)

BROWN: No, no, don't you. (*Picks up cases.*) There's nothing the matter with me . . .

(BROWN *follows the* NURSE *inside. The* DOCTOR *watches them go, picks up Brown's form, and reads it. Then he picks up the phone and starts to dial.*)

SCENE 2

Brown's private ward. A pleasant ward with a hospital bed and the usual furniture. One wall is almost all window and is curtained.
BROWN *and the* NURSE *enter.* BROWN *puts his cases on the bed. He likes the room.*

BROWN: That's nice. I'll like it here. (*Peering through curtains*) What's the view?

NURSE: Well, it's the drive and the gardens.

BROWN: Gardens. A front room. What could be nicer?

(NURSE *starts to open case.*)

NURSE: Are your night things in here?

BROWN: Yes, I'll be very happy here.

169

(NURSE *opens the case, which is full of money—banknotes.*)

NURSE: Oh—I'm sorry—

(BROWN *is not put out at all.*)

BROWN: What time is breakfast?

NURSE: Eight o'clock.

BROWN: Lunch?

NURSE: Twelve o'clock.

BROWN: Tea?

NURSE: Three o'clock.

BROWN: Supper?

NURSE: Half-past six.

BROWN: Cocoa?

NURSE: Nine.

BROWN: Like clockwork. Lovely.

(*The* DOCTOR *enters with Brown's form and an adhesive bandage.*)

DOCTOR: Excuse me.

BROWN: I was just saying—everything's A1.

DOCTOR: I remembered your finger.

BROWN: I'd forgotten myself. It's nothing.

DOCTOR: Well, we'll just put this on overnight.

(*He puts on the adhesive strip.*)

I expect Matron will be along to discuss your case with you tomorrow.

BROWN: My finger?

DOCTOR: . . . Well, I expect she'd like to meet you.

BROWN: Be pleased to meet her.

SCENE 3

The hospital office. It is morning, and the DOCTOR *is at the desk, telephoning.*

DOCTOR: . . . I have absolutely no idea . . . The nurse said it looked like rather a lot . . . His savings, yes. No, I don't really want the police turning up at the bedside of any patient who doesn't arrive with a life history . . . I think we'd get more out of him than you would, given a little time . . . No, he's not being difficult at all . . . You don't need to worry about that—he seems quite happy . . .

Brown's private ward. BROWN *is in striped pyjamas, eating off a tray. A second nurse—*NURSE COATES (MAGGIE)—*is waiting for him to finish so that she can take his tray away.* MAGGIE *is pretty and warm.*

BROWN: The point is not breakfast in bed, but breakfast in bed without guilt—if you're not ill. Lunch in bed is more difficult, even for the rich. It's not any more expensive, but the disapproval is harder to ignore. To stay in bed for tea is almost impossible in decent society, and not to get up at all would probably bring in the authorities. But in a hospital it's not only understood—it's expected. That's the beauty of it. I'm not saying it's a great discovery—it's obvious really: but I'd say I'd got something.

MAGGIE: If you'd got something, there wouldn't be all this fuss.

BROWN: Is there a fuss?

(MAGGIE *doesn't answer.*)

I'm paying my way . . . Are you pretty full all the time?

MAGGIE: Not at the moment, not very.

BROWN: You'd think a place as nice as this would be very popular.

MAGGIE: Popular?

BROWN: I thought I might have to wait for a place, you know.

MAGGIE: Where do you live?

BROWN: I've never lived. Only stayed.

MAGGIE: You should settle down somewhere.

BROWN: Yes, I've been promising myself this.

MAGGIE: Have you got a family?

BROWN: I expect so.

MAGGIE: Where are they?

BROWN: I lost touch.

MAGGIE: You should find them.

BROWN: (*Smiles.*) Their name's Brown.

(*The* MATRON *enters: she is not too old, and quite pleasant.*)

MATRON: Good morning.

BROWN: Good morning to you. You must be Matron.

MATRON: That's right.

BROWN: I must congratulate you on your hospital, it's a lovely place you run here. Everyone is so nice.

MATRON: Well, thank you, Mr Brown. I'm glad you feel at home.

(MAGGIE *takes* BROWN's *tray*.)

BROWN: I never felt it there. Very good breakfast. Just what the doctor ordered. I hope he got a bit of a lie-in.

(MAGGIE *exits with the tray, closing the door*.)

MATRON: Now, what's your problem, Mr Brown?

BROWN: I have no problems.

MATRON: Your complaint.

BROWN: I have no complaints either. Full marks.

MATRON: Most people who come here have something the *matter* with them.

BROWN: That must give you a lot of extra work.

MATRON: But it's what we're here for. You see, you can't really stay unless there's something wrong with you.

BROWN: I can pay.

MATRON: That's not the point.

BROWN: What is the point?

MATRON: This is a hospital. What are you after?

BROWN: (*Sadly*) My approach is too straightforward. An ordinary malingerer or a genuine hypochondriac wouldn't have all this trouble. They'd be accepted on their own terms. All I get is a lot of personal questions. (*Hopefully*) Maybe I could *catch* something . . . But what difference would it make to you?

MATRON: We have to keep the beds free for people who need them.

BROWN: I need this room.

MATRON: I believe you, Mr Brown—but wouldn't another room like this one do?—somewhere else? You see, we deal with physical matters—of the body—

BROWN: There's nothing wrong with my *mind*. You won't find my name on any list.

MATRON: I know.

BROWN: (*Teasing*) How do you know?

(*She doesn't answer*.)

Go for the obvious, it's worth considering. I know what I like: a nice atmosphere—good food—clean rooms—no demands—cheerful staff—Well, it's *worth* the price. I won't be any trouble.

MATRON: Have you thought of going to a nice country hotel?

BROWN: Different kettle of fish altogether. I want to do nothing, and have nothing expected of me. That isn't possible out there. It worries them. They want to know what you're at—staying in your room all the time—they want to know what you're *doing*. But in a hospital it is understood that you're not doing anything, because everybody's in the same boat—it's the normal thing.

MATRON: But there's nothing wrong with you!

BROWN: That's why I'm *here*. If there was something wrong with me I could get into any old hospital—free. As it is, I'm quite happy to pay for *not* having anything wrong with me.

MATRON: But what do you want to do here?

BROWN: Nothing.

MATRON: You'll find that very boring.

BROWN: One must expect to be bored, in a hospital.

MATRON: Have you been in a hospital quite a lot?

BROWN: No. I've been saving up for it . . . (*He smiles.*)

SCENE 5

The hospital office. The DOCTOR *is phoning at a desk.*

DOCTOR: No luck? . . . Oh. Well, I don't know. The only plan we've got is to bore him out of here, but he's disturbingly self-sufficient . . . Mmmm, we've had a psychiatrist over . . . Well, he seemed amused . . . Both of them, actually; they were both amused . . . No, I shouldn't do that, he won't tell you anything. And there's one of our nurses—she's getting on very well with him . . . something's bound to come out soon . . .

SCENE 6

Brown's ward. BROWN *is in bed with a thermometer in his mouth.* MAGGIE *is taking his pulse. She removes the thermometer, scans it and shakes it.*

MAGGIE: I'm wasting my time here, you know.

BROWN: (*Disappointed*) Normal?

MAGGIE: You'll have to do better than that if you're going to stay.

BROWN: You're breaking my heart, Maggie.

MAGGIE: (*Almost lovingly*) Brownie, what are you going to do with yourself?

BROWN: Maggie, Maggie . . . Why do you want me to do something?

MAGGIE: They've all got theories about you, you know.

BROWN: Theories?

MAGGIE: Train robber.

BROWN: That's a good one.

MAGGIE: Embezzler.

BROWN: Naturally.

MAGGIE: Eccentric millionaire.

BROWN: Wish I was. I'd have my own hospital, just for myself— with nurses, doctors, rubber floors, flowers, stretchers parked by the elevators, clean towels and fire regulations . . .

MAGGIE: It's generally agreed you're on the run.

BROWN: No, I've stopped.

MAGGIE: I think you're just lazy.

BROWN: I knew you were the clever one.

MAGGIE: (*Troubled, soft*) Tell me what's the matter, Brownie?

BROWN: I would if there was.

MAGGIE: What do you want to stay here for then?

BROWN: I like you.

MAGGIE: You didn't know I was here.

BROWN: That's true. I came for the quiet and the routine. I came for the white calm, meals on trays and quiet efficiency, time passing and bringing nothing. That seemed enough. I never got it down to a person. But I like you—I like you very much.

MAGGIE: Well, I like you too, Brownie. But there's more in life than that.

(MATRON *enters.*)

MATRON: Good morning.

BROWN: Good morning, Matron.

MATRON: And how are we this morning?

BROWN: We're very well. How are you?

MATRON: (*Slightly taken aback*) I'm all right, thank you. Well, are you enjoying life?

BROWN: Yes, thank you, Matron.

MATRON: What have you been doing?

BROWN: Nothing.

MATRON: Now really, Mr Brown, this won't do, you know.

174

Wouldn't you like to get up for a while? Have a walk in the garden? There's no reason why you shouldn't.

BROWN: No, I suppose not. But I didn't come here for that. I must have walked thousands of miles, in my time.

MATRON: It's not healthy to stay in bed all day.

BROWN: What do the other patients do?

MATRON: The other patients are here because they are not well.

BROWN: I thought patients did things . . . (*Vaguely*) made things.

MATRON: I suppose you wouldn't like to make paper flowers?

BROWN: What on earth for? You've got lots of real ones.

MATRON: *You* haven't got any.

BROWN: Well, no one knows I'm here.

MATRON: Then you must tell somebody.

BROWN: I don't want them to know.

MATRON: Who?

BROWN: Everybody.

MATRON: You'll soon get tired of sitting in bed.

BROWN: Then I'll sit by the window. I'm easily pleased.

MATRON: I can't let you just languish away in here. You must do *something*.

BROWN: (*Sighs*.) All right. What?

MATRON: We've got basket-weaving . . . ?

BROWN: Then I'll be left alone, will I?

SCENE 7

The hospital office. The DOCTOR *is on the phone.*

DOCTOR: Well, *I* don't know—how many John Browns *are* there in Somerset House? . . . Good grief! . . . Of course, if it's any consolation it may not be his real name . . . I know it doesn't help . . . That's an idea, yes . . . His fingerprints . . . No, no, I'll get them on a glass or something—Well, he might have been in trouble some time . . .

SCENE 8

Brown's ward. BROWN *is working on a shapeless piece of basketry.*
MATRON *enters.*

MATRON: What is it?

BROWN: Basketwork.

MATRON: But what is it for?

BROWN: Therapy.

MATRON: You're making fun of me.

BROWN: It is functional on one level only. If that. *You'd* like me to make a sort of laundry basket and lower myself in it out of the window. That would be functional on *two* levels. At least. (*Regards the mess sadly.*) And I'm not even blind.

(MATRON *silently dispossesses* BROWN *of his basketry.*)

MATRON: What about *painting*, Mr Brown.

(*That strikes a chord.*)

BROWN: Painting . . . I used to do a bit of painting.

MATRON: Splendid. Would you do some for me?

BROWN: Paint in here?

MATRON: Nurse Coates will bring you materials.

BROWN: What colours do you like?

MATRON: I like all colours. Just paint what you fancy. Paint scenes from your own life.

BROWN: Clever! Should I paint my last place of employment?

MATRON: I'm trying to help you.

BROWN: I'm sorry. I know you are. But I don't need help. Everything's fine for me. (*Pause.*) Would you like me to paint the countryside?

MATRON: Yes, that would be nice.

SCENE 9

The hospital office. The DOCTOR *is on the phone.*

DOCTOR: No . . . well, we haven't got anything against him really. He's not doing any *harm*. No, he pays regularly. We can't really refuse . . . He's got lots left . . .

SCENE 10

Brown's ward. BROWN *is painting a landscape all over one wall. He hasn't got very far, but one sees the beginnings of a simple pastoral scene, competent but amateurish.* MAGGIE *enters, carrying cut flowers in a vase.*

MAGGIE: Hello—(*She notices.*)

BROWN: I'll need some more paint.

MAGGIE: (*Horrified*) Brownie! I gave you drawing paper!

176

BROWN: I like space. I like the big sweep—the contours of hills all flowing.

MAGGIE: Matron will have a fit.

BROWN: What are the flowers?

MAGGIE: You don't deserve them.

BROWN: Who are they from?

MAGGIE: Me.

BROWN: Maggie!

MAGGIE: I didn't buy them.

BROWN: Pinched them?

MAGGIE: Picked them.

BROWN: A lovely thought. Put them over there. I should bring *you* flowers.

MAGGIE: I'm not ill.

BROWN: Nor am I. Do you like it?

MAGGIE: Very pretty.

BROWN: I'm only doing it to please Matron really. I could do with a bigger brush. There's more paint, is there? I'll need a lot of blue. It's going to be summer in here.

MAGGIE: It's summer outside. Isn't that good enough for you?
   (BROWN *stares out of the window: gardens, flowers, trees, hills.*)

BROWN: I couldn't stay out there. You don't get the benefits.

MAGGIE: (*Leaving*) I'll have to tell Matron, you know.

BROWN: You don't get the looking after. And the privacy. (*He considers.*) I'll have to take the curtains down.

SCENE 11

The hospital office.

MATRON: What did the psychiatrist think?

DOCTOR: He likes him.

MATRON: (*Sour*) He's likeable.

DOCTOR: (*Thoughtfully*) I just thought I'd let him stay the night. I wanted to go back to bed and it seemed the easiest thing to do. I thought that in the morning . . . Well, I'm not sure what I thought would happen in the morning.

MATRON: He's not simple—he's giving nothing away. Not even to Nurse Coates.

DOCTOR: Well, keep her at it.

MATRON: She doesn't need much keeping.

Brown's ward. BROWN *has painted a whole wall and is working on a second one.* MAGGIE *sits on the bed.*

MAGGIE: That was when I started nursing, after that.

BROWN: Funny. I would have thought your childhood was all to do with ponies and big stone-floored kitchens . . .

MAGGIE: Goes to show. What was your childhood like?

BROWN: Young . . . I wish I had more money.

MAGGIE: You've got a lot. You must have had a good job . . . ?

BROWN: Centre forward for Arsenal.

MAGGIE: You're not fair! You don't give me anything in return.

BROWN: This painting's for you, Maggie . . . If I'd got four times as much money, I'd take four rooms and paint one for each season. But I've only got money for the summer.

MAGGIE: What will you do when it's gone?

BROWN: (*Seriously*) I don't know. Perhaps I'll get ill and have to go to a hospital. But I'll miss you, Maggie.

MAGGIE: If you had someone to look after you you wouldn't have this trouble.

BROWN: What trouble?

MAGGIE: If you had someone to cook your meals and do your laundry you'd be all right, wouldn't you?

BROWN: It's the things that go with it.

MAGGIE: You should have got married. I bet you had chances.

BROWN: Perhaps.

MAGGIE: It's not too late.

BROWN: You don't think so?

MAGGIE: You're attractive.

BROWN: What are you like when you're not in uniform? I can't think of you not being a nurse. It belongs to another world I'm not part of any more.

MAGGIE: What have you got about hospitals?

BROWN: A hospital is a very dependable place. Anything could be going on outside. Since I've been in here—there could be a war on, and for once it's got nothing to do with me. I don't even know about it. Fire, flood and misery of all kinds, across the world or over the hill, it can all go on, but this is a private ward; I'm paying for it. (*Pause.*) The meals come in

178

on trays, on the dot—the dust never settles before it's wiped—clean laundry at the appointed time—the matron does her round, not affected by anything outside. You need never know anything, it doesn't touch you.

MAGGIE: That's not true, Brownie.

BROWN: I know it's not.

MAGGIE: Then you shouldn't try and make it true.

BROWN: I know I shouldn't.

(*Pause.*)

MAGGIE: Is that all there is to it, then?

BROWN: You've still got theories?

MAGGIE: There's a new one. You're a retired forger.

BROWN: Ha! The money's real enough.

MAGGIE: I know.

BROWN: How do you know?

MAGGIE: (*Shamefaced*) They had it checked.

(BROWN *laughs.*)

BROWN: They've got to make it difficult. I've got to be a crook or a lunatic.

MAGGIE: Then why don't you tell them where you came from?

BROWN: They want to pass me on. But they don't know who to, or where. I'm happy here.

MAGGIE: Haven't you been happy anywhere else?

BROWN: Yes. I had a good four years of it once.

MAGGIE: In hospital?

BROWN: No, that was abroad.

MAGGIE: Where have you been?

BROWN: All over. I've been among French, Germans, Greeks, Turks, Arabs . . .

MAGGIE: What were you doing?

BROWN: Different things in different places. (*Smiles.*) I was painting in France.

MAGGIE: An artist?

BROWN: Oh very. Green and brown. I could turn a row of tanks into a leafy hedgerow. Not literally. Worse luck.

SCENE 13

The hospital office. The DOCTOR *is on the phone.*

DOCTOR: . . . He meant camouflage . . . Well, I realize that, but
there are a number of points to narrow the field . . . Must be
records of some kind . . . Service in France and Germany,
probably Middle East . . .

SCENE 14

Brown's ward. BROWN *has painted two walls and is working on a third.*

MAGGIE: It's very nice, Brownie. Perhaps you'll be famous and
people will come here to see your mural.

BROWN: I wouldn't let them in.

MAGGIE: After you're dead. In a hundred years.

'BROWN: Yes, they could come in then.

MAGGIE: What will you do when you've finished the room?

BROWN: Go back to bed. It'll be nice in here. Hospital routine in a
pastoral setting. That's kind of perfection, really.

MAGGIE: You could have put your bed in the garden.

BROWN: What's the date?

MAGGIE: The twenty-seventh.

BROWN: I've lasted well, haven't I?

MAGGIE: How old are you?

BROWN: Twice your age.

MAGGIE: Forty-four?

BROWN: And more. (*Looking close*) What are you thinking?

MAGGIE: Before I was born, you were in the war.

BROWN: (*Moves.*) Yes. Private Brown.

MAGGIE: Was it awful being in the war?

BROWN: I didn't like the first bit. But in the end it was very nice.

MAGGIE: What happened to you?

BROWN: I got taken prisoner . . . Four years.

MAGGIE: Is that when you were happy?

BROWN: Yes . . . Funny thing, that camp. Up to then it was all
terrible. Chaos—all the pins must have fallen off the map,
dive bombers and bullets. Oh dear, yes. The camp was like
breathing out for the first time in months. I couldn't believe it.
It was like winning, being captured. The war was still going on
but I wasn't going to it any more. They gave us food, life was

180

regulated, in a box of earth and wire and sky. On my second
day I knew what it reminded me of.

MAGGIE: What?

BROWN: Here. It reminded me of here.

SCENE 15

The hospital office. Present are the DOCTOR, MATRON *and* MAGGIE.
The DOCTOR *holding a big book—a record of admissions, his finger on
a line.*

DOCTOR: John Brown. And an address. (*To* MAGGIE) Well done.

MAGGIE: (*Troubled*) But does it make any difference?

MATRON: What was he doing round here?

DOCTOR: Staying with relatives—or holiday, we can find out.

MATRON: So long ago?

DOCTOR: Compound fracture—car accident. The driver paid for
    him . . . Well, something to go on at last!

MAGGIE: He hasn't done anything wrong, has he?

SCENE 16

Brown's ward. The painting nearly covers the walls. BROWN *is finishing
it off in one corner.*

BROWN: I was a regular, you see, and peace didn't match up to the
    war I'd had. There was too much going on.

MAGGIE: So what did you do then?

BROWN: This and that. Didn't fancy a lot. (*He paints.*) Shouldn't
    you be working, or something?

MAGGIE: I'll go if you like.

BROWN: I like you being here. Just wondered.

MAGGIE: Wondered what?

BROWN: I'm telling you about myself, aren't I? I shouldn't put you
    in that position—if they find out they'll blame you for not
    passing it on.

MAGGIE: But you haven't done anything wrong, have you,
    Brownie?

BROWN: Is that what you're here for?

MAGGIE: No.

    (BROWN *finishes off the painting and stands back.*)

BROWN: There.

MAGGIE: It's lovely.

BROWN: Yes. Quite good. It'll be nice, to sit here inside my painting. I'll enjoy that.

SCENE 17

The hospital office. The DOCTOR *is on the phone.*

DOCTOR: . . . Brown. John Brown—yes, he was here before, a long time ago—we've got him in the records—Mmm—and an address. We'll start checking . . . there must be *somebody* . . .

SCENE 18

Brown's ward. The walls are covered with paintings. BROWN *is sitting on the bed. The door opens and a strange nurse—*NURSE JONES— *enters with Brown's lunch on a tray.*

JONES: Are you ready for lunch—? (*Sees the painting.*) My, my, aren't you clever—it's better than anyone would have thought.

BROWN: Where's Maggie?

JONES: Nurse Coates? I don't know.

BROWN: But—she's my nurse.

JONES: Yours? Well, she's everybody's.

BROWN: (*Worried*) You don't understand—she's looking after *me*, you see.

(*The* DOCTOR *enters;* NURSE JONES *leaves.*)

DOCTOR: (*Cheerful*) Well, Mr Brown, good news.

BROWN: (*Wary*) Yes?

DOCTOR: You're going to have visitors.

BROWN: Visitors?

DOCTOR: Your sister Mabel and her husband. They were amazed to hear from you.

BROWN: They didn't hear from *me*.

DOCTOR: They're travelling up tomorrow. All your friends had been wondering where you'd got to—

BROWN: Where's Nurse Coates gone?

DOCTOR: Nowhere. She's round about. I think she's on nights downstairs this week. I understand that you were here once before—as a child.

BROWN: Yes. (*Angrily*) You couldn't leave well alone, could you?
DOCTOR: (*Pause; not phony any more*) It's not enough, Mr Brown.
You've got to . . . *connect* . . .

SCENE 19

The hospital office. BROWN *appears, dressed, carrying his bags, from the direction of his room. He sees* MAGGIE *and stops. She sees him.*
MAGGIE: Brownie! Where are you going?
BROWN: Back.
MAGGIE: Back where?
(*He does not answer.*)
You blame me?
BROWN: No. No. I don't *really*. You had to tell them, didn't you?
MAGGIE: I'm sorry—I—
BROWN: You thought it was for the best.
MAGGIE: Yes, I did. I still do. It's not good for you, what you're doing.
BROWN: How do you know?—*you* mean it wouldn't be good for *you*. How do you know what's good for me?
MAGGIE: They're coming tomorrow. Family, friends; isn't that good?
BROWN: I could have found them, if I'd wanted. I didn't come here for that. (*Comes up to her.*) They won. (*Looks out through the front doors.*) I feel I should breathe in before going out there.
MAGGIE: I can't let you go, Brownie.
BROWN: (*Gently mocking*) Regulations?
MAGGIE: I can't.
BROWN: I'm free to come and go. I'm paying.
MAGGIE: I know—but it *is* a hospital.
BROWN: (*Smiles briefly.*) I'm not ill. Don't wake the doctor, he doesn't like being woken. (*Moves.*) Don't be sorry—I had a good time here with you. Do you think they'll leave my painting?
MAGGIE: Brownie . . .
BROWN: Trouble is, I've always been so *well*. If I'd been *sick* I would have been all right.
(*He goes out into the night.*)